She'd never known love could burn so hot . . .

Emily looked up at Jacob, her smile radiant with the passion she'd felt for him for too long. "I've wanted you so much," she whispered.

"You've been driving me out of my mind for the past two years. Did you know that?" He struggled briefly with the catch on her bra and watched, enraptured, as the silk fell away to reveal her breasts. He touched one of her nipples, and excitement coursed through him as it grew taut, more evidence of her response to him.

"No, Jacob, I had no idea. And no idea how good you'd make me feel."

He bent to kiss her tenderly. "Two years ago, everything was wrong for us," he murmured, enclosing her in his embrace. "But this time around, it's going to be right. It's going to be perfect. . . ."

Jayne Ann Krentz weaves two themes into this enchanting story—that of a woman gaining the courage to take charge of her own life, and that of a couple who knew each other at the wrong time meeting again. Years later, the time is right for love to reach full bloom.

The heroine's assertiveness training course has significance for Jayne, who benefited from taking one herself. This very talented and popular author, also published as Stephanie James and Jayne Castle, has written more than forty books. She and her husband live in Seattle, Washington.

Books by Jayne Ann Krentz

Don't miss any of our special offers. Write to us at the following address for information on our newest releases.

Harlequin Reader Service
901 Fuhrmann Blvd., P.O. Box 1397, Buffalo, NY 14240
Canadian address: P.O. Box 603,
Fort Erie, Ont. L2A 5X3

Full Bloom

JAYNE ANN KRENTZ

Harlequin Books

TORONTO • NEW YORK • LONDON
AMSTERDAM • PARIS • SYDNEY • HAMBURG
STOCKHOLM • ATHENS • TOKYO • MILAN

Published February 1988

ISBN 0-373-25291-9

1

ALL THINGS CONSIDERED, Emily Ravenscroft thought, she was taking the news of the outcome of her latest folly much better than she had the last time. She was wryly proud of herself. No tears, no rush of despair, no hysterical protests. Her assertiveness training class instructor would have been proud of her.

Emily took the news and kept on smiling.

It wasn't much of a smile, just a faint, ironic curve of her mouth, but it was enough to conceal the pain and the anger that were simmering inside.

It was also enough of a smile to thoroughly alarm three of the four people who confronted her in her father's study. She could not see what effect her smile had on the fourth person in the room. He was standing apart from the others, a dark, brooding figure concealed in shadows.

Jacob Stone was a man who was at home in shadows.

Ever since Emily had first become aware of his existence five years ago, she had understood that he prowled the fringes of her family's world. He was part bodyguard, part troubleshooter and, to Emily's way of thinking, part enforcer for Ravenscroft International. Like the last of the lobo wolves, he was rarely seen in broad daylight, let alone in the firm's executive suites or at its glittering social functions. And the only times he had been invited into her father's private study were on those occasions when Emily had needed rescuing from her latest predicament. The Ravenscrofts preferred to keep family problems quiet, and Jacob Stone could be relied on to do a job and keep family secrets to himself.

Emily had not seen Jacob Stone in nearly two years. It had been a shock to find him here at her parents' home this evening. She had assumed he was still abroad.

But it was an even bigger shock to discover that the passion she had first experienced for him five years ago had not died, after all. It had only gone dormant. Seeing Jacob again tonight had been like pouring rain and sunlight on fertile soil. Emily could literally feel the seeds of her old love sprouting again.

Don't be stupid, she told herself fiercely. *You've got problems enough without letting yourself get sucked back into a young, immature woman's fantasy.* She was twenty-seven years old now, and she had changed.

Emily didn't waste any time trying to guess how Jacob was reacting to her unexpected calm. She knew enough about him to realize that no one would ever understand him unless he wished it, and that was highly unlikely. He was a man who operated alone, working by his own rules even when he was doing a job for his employers. Emily thought of him in the same way she thought of hurricanes, charging lions and marauding sharks. The only sensible thing to do when any of them was in the vicinity was to get out of the way.

But sometimes one could not avoid acts of nature. They descended with the inevitability of fate.

She had not had a close look at Jacob Stone since she had so innocently walked into the study twenty minutes earlier, but she remembered him well enough from two years ago when she had last seen him. He would not have changed much. Chunks of granite did not alter greatly in short spans of time. It took aeons to modify even slightly the face of a rock cliff. Jacob Stone would probably look much the same forty years from now as he had two years ago.

Without looking at him, Emily knew he would still have those cold, emotionless gray eyes and those harsh, unyielding features. He would still be wearing his tawny brown hair in a short, almost military style. His body would still be lean and hard and solid, too, Emily suspected. Stone had more than enough self-discipline to keep himself from getting soft. He would be thirty-seven by now. Tougher and more intimidating than ever.

And, she decided in a flash of affectionate amusement, he would still look vaguely uncomfortable in a suit. Jacob Stone frequently wore a suit and tie when he was working for Ravenscroft International, but he would never really look at home in the traditional businessman's outfit. Putting a suit and tie on Stone was a little like dressing up any large, wild beast. Even if the tie was silk and the suit Italian, you couldn't disguise the fact that what was underneath was still big and dangerous and had a set of teeth. —

The tape in the recording machine sitting on Gifford Ravenscroft's desk hissed into silence. Emily stared at the small, sleek tape player and tried to hate Jacob Stone for what he had done this evening. He was the one who had supplied the tape to her father. It wasn't the first time Stone had stepped into her world and rearranged things with a heavy hand. She tried to tell herself that her past fantasies about him were just that: fantasies. The truth was, Jacob Stone was a very unlikable man. A hard, ruthless, unrelenting man.

"Well, Emily," Gifford said quietly, "you've managed to get yourself into trouble again. Do you understand now why I asked you to come here today?"

Emily forced herself to take three deep breaths before she answered. The first rule of assertiveness was to stay calm and in control. Then she arched her eyebrows above the frames of her round glasses and scanned the concerned faces of her mother, Catherine, and her older brother, Drake, before she met her father's stern gaze. She ignored Stone, who had still not moved in the shadows.

"Let me guess," she said with artificial lightness. "You didn't invite me here to discuss the loan I've requested, right?"

"Emily!" Catherine stared at her daughter, appalled. "What's the matter with you? This is a very serious situation. According to this tape you are about to announce your engagement to a man who plans to use you to take control of Ravenscroft International. Your father has outlined the evidence Jacob has gathered for us. This is not a joking matter. You must put an end to your relationship with Damon Morrell immediately."

Emily gritted her teeth and kept her faint smile in place. She looked at her mother. Catherine Ravenscroft was nearing sixty, but she was still a striking woman who managed to look at least fifteen years younger than her age. Although she was a Ravenscroft by marriage, not by blood, she had the family coloring. Her smoothly coiffed hair had once been jet black. Now it was artfully streaked with silver.

Catherine had brown eyes, too, which, if not exactly the true amber of a Ravenscroft's gaze, were close enough to fool most observers. Altogether she fitted in very well with the others. Her family had lost its considerable fortune somewhere along the way years ago, but along with her striking features, Catherine had also brought a good old-stock pedigree into the family. She was very conscious of her background and rigidly determined that Emily, her unexpected late-in-life daughter, make a marriage that suited what she saw as Emily's position in the world.

Tonight Emily's mother was dressed with her usual elegantly casual flair in a pair of khaki silk pants and a cream-colored blouse. There was a delicate rope of gold and diamonds around her throat.

Emily struggled to recall the techniques she had learned in her assertiveness training class. *Do not argue. Do not provide a target that can be attacked.*

"You and Dad and Drake have all gone to a great deal of effort, and I assure you I'm quite impressed." Emily transferred her smile to her black-haired older brother and then to her father. "It's obvious you all put in a lot of time on this project, and I'm quite flattered that you once again felt it necessary to call in Mr. Stone to do the dirty work. I realize his time is quite expensive. But then, I suspect he enjoys this sort of job."

There was a soft gasp of annoyance from Catherine Ravenscroft, and Drake's amber eyes flickered assessingly. Stone himself did not bother to react to the insult. But Gifford Ravenscroft glared at his daughter. It was obvious he was angry, but it was equally clear he was somewhat perplexed. He had not been prepared for this cool flippancy from the daughter he had always thought of as naïve and emotional.

"Your mother is right, Emily. This is no time for jokes or insults. Your relationship with Morrell must be terminated immediately. The man is not interested in you. That tape and the accompanying evidence demonstrate that beyond a shadow of a doubt. His only interest is in taking control of Ravenscroft International or crippling the firm. He plans to do that by marrying you. Why

Mother took it into her head on her deathbed to leave you enough shares to ensure you a seat on RI's board of directors will always be a mystery to me."

"She must have been out of her mind," Catherine said with a sigh. "But she always was a bit strange, what with her unbusinesslike ideas about how to run things."

"Calm down, Dad," Emily said, deliberately trying for a tone of careless amusement. Her grandmother had died almost two years ago, shortly after Jacob Stone had left for a foreign office of RI. It had been a turning point in Emily's life. Her grandmother was the only Ravenscroft Emily felt had ever really understood her. She had loved the old woman. "I've always let you and Drake and Mother control my vote, haven't I? I've never tried to interfere with the running of the firm. I don't even take any income from the shares Grandmother left me. I let the money be reinvested in the firm, just as Grandmother stated in her will. Nothing would change even if I did decide to marry Damon."

She couldn't resist the taunt, and the startled faces of her family was more than enough of a reaction to satisfy her. Until recently Emily had always bowed to the wishes of the family. The truth was, she had never intended to marry Damon, but she was not about to let the rest of her family know that tonight. Emily was surrounded, and she did not intend to give up what little ammunition she had. Let the others sweat a bit. It would do them good.

It was Drake who responded first. He was a striking man with black hair and the Ravenscroft eyes. He was ten years older than his sister and knew her better than her parents ever would. He was the chief executive officer of RI, the man responsible for day-to-day operations, but he did not perform his duties in isolation. Gifford Ravenscroft still took a very active interest in the running of the family business, as did Catherine. Privately Emily considered her brother something of a genius as well as a diplomat, to be able to hold the reins of power and placate his parents at the same time. The fact that he was here at their parents' home this evening was ample proof that he considered the situation as serious as they did.

Drake leaned back in his chair, his hands folded under his strong chin as he studied Emily. "Don't be deliberately naïve, Em. You pay very little attention to the daily business of the company, but that doesn't mean Morrell would be just as uninterested. We know for a fact he's very interested. It wouldn't take much for him to throw a monkey wrench into things by using you. He could destroy this company. You'd probably start voting the way he wanted you to vote, believing he loved you and only had your best interests at heart."

"And I assure you," Gifford continued ominously, "that Morrell would use you to cause as much disruption as possible for all of us. He has a vendetta against Ravenscroft International. He would do anything he could to destroy us."

"Why?" Emily could not resist asking. She felt like a flower being hammered beneath a driving rain. Her family was united in the effort to bring her to heel.

All the while Jacob Stone stood in the shadows near the window, witnessing the unequal battle. He was just the soldier who had completed his assigned mission. It was up to the Ravenscrofts to bring Emily into line.

"There's no point in going into the whole tale tonight," Gifford snapped. "It has to do with an incident that took place a couple of years ago. A business matter, pure and simple. Suffice it to say that RI submitted the winning bid and Morrell's firm lost out. Morrell swore he'd get even. We're going up against him again right now. We're competing with him on the Fowler project. He'd like very much to get rid of the competition and take his revenge against us at the same time. Destroying RI from within is his idea of vengeance. He's using you, Emily. Don't you understand?"

Emily forced her smile up another notch in brilliance. "Have you considered that you may have that backward?"

"What the hell are you talking about?" Drake demanded coolly.

"Maybe I'm using Damon." Emily smoothed the skirt of her yellow knit dress. "He's a very interesting man, you know. Handsome, successful, attentive. An excellent conversationalist. What's more, he says he likes flowers."

Catherine frowned severely as she always did at the mention of flowers. She had never accepted the fact that her daughter owned a florist's shop. "You're being deliberately difficult tonight. Why, Emily? You've heard the evidence Jacob collected. How can you sit there and act like this?"

"Would you prefer that I break down in tears the way I did two years ago when you decided to get rid of my first fiancé?" Emily asked.

"Emily, no one wants you in tears," Catherine said impatiently. "Why must you always assume we're deliberately picking on you when all we really want is what's best for you? We want you to understand what's going on here. Jacob has proved beyond a shadow of a doubt that Morrell is not interested in you. He's only interested in Ravenscroft International. You can't deny the evidence you've heard tonight."

For the first time Emily allowed her gaze to move into the shadows. She met Jacob Stone's eyes. "Tapes can be faked. Everyone knows that. Why should I believe the one Mr. Stone has put together?"

Drake stirred abruptly. Obviously no one had expected her to question the evidence. "You know better than that, Emily. Jacob wouldn't have faked that tape."

Emily looked at her brother, the anger within her simmering to the surface for the first time. "Jacob Stone would do anything you or Father told him to do. He works for you. Yes, I realize he carries a fancy title. Vice president in charge of overseas operations or some such thing, but we all know the truth, don't we? He's nothing more than your paid enforcer. He's a professional intimidator. Why should I believe anything he put together for this little confrontation?"

No one in the room seemed to know how to react to the savage insult. Emily tried to take some satisfaction from that small victory. It was not often she was able to score even a tiny win from her family. She did not dare look back at Jacob to see how he had responded.

"Jacob is a man of honor," Gifford Ravenscroft finally said with a grimness that emphasized how hard he was working to keep control of his temper. "And for your information, he resigned his position with RI two months ago. He is here tonight as a favor."

"Is that right?" Emily asked with false brightness. "He just does this sort of work now for the fun of it?" She sent a scathing glance into the shadows of the room. Stone did not move. He just stood there quietly watching her. His very stillness was unnerving.

"Dammit, Emily, stop attacking Jacob," Drake ordered. "He helped us out on this, and we're grateful. We didn't want an outsider doing the investigation. We can count on Jacob to keep his mouth shut. None of this will go any farther than this room."

"How reassuring," Emily said dryly. "I hate to break this to you, but I'm not particularly worried about how far this goes."

"Emily, dear, there's no need to be sarcastic. I realize this is upsetting for you," Catherine interjected more gently. "But you must realize we're only doing this for your own good. You don't understand big business; nor do you understand what kind of man Morrell is. He's a conniving bastard. He'll use anyone or anything, and unfortunately he's decided to use you. Now that you know the truth, we expect you to be sensible about this. You must put an end to the relationship. It's very dangerous. You can't possibly marry the man."

Emily decided she'd had enough. She collected her small leather purse and got to her feet. The members of her family stared at her in astonishment.

"It's been a very interesting evening," she assured them all brightly. "I was looking forward to staying for dinner, but under the circumstances, I hope you'll excuse me."

"Sit down, Emily!" Gifford roared. "We're not through here."

Emily ignored him. It was the first time she had ever done such a thing. She walked to the door. "I've got a long drive ahead of me. I'd better be on my way."

"Emily!" her mother exclaimed. "You can't be serious. It's much too late to drive back to Seattle tonight. That's a two-hundred-mile trip. You won't get home until nearly midnight."

"All the more reason to be moving along," Emily said cheerfully from the door. She had her hand on the knob. It was turning beneath her fingers. In another moment she would be free. "Thanks for the invitation to spend the weekend, but I'll have to take a rain check. I'm sure you can understand that I've lost some of my enthusiasm for family life. Good night, everyone."

She was through the door, closing it behind her. Emily realized she was almost shaking in reaction. But she was all right, she assured herself. She had survived. She was not going to dissolve into anguished tears the way she had two years ago when she had been summoned to her father's study to learn the truth about the man she had been planning to marry. Maybe it was easier this time around because she had never planned to marry Damon Morrell. Emily did not plan to marry anyone, ever. But her family did not know that.

Clutching her purse with whitened knuckles, Emily walked determinedly across the oriental carpets and polished hardwood floors of her parents' elegant Portland hillside home. Then she let herself out into the chill of the spring night. The Oregon skies still leaked rain as she slid into her small compact. It was probably wet all the way from here to Seattle, she thought. It was going to be a long drive.

Emily sat behind the wheel for a moment, composing herself. It was hard to tell which of the fierce emotions raging within her was dominant. Humiliation mixed with fury was a powerful combination.

But by far the harshest emotion she was experiencing was generated by the realization that after all this time she still loved Jacob Stone. That fact jolted her far more terribly than anything she had heard on the tape that damned Morrell.

Emily had been so sure she had shed her hopeless passion for Jacob along with so many of the other naïve dreams she had entertained in the past. So sure she had finally grown up. But apparently part of her was destined to remain naïve forever.

She wanted to dash off into the safety of the night, but common sense told her she had to calm down a little before she turned the key in the ignition.

A SHOCKED SILENCE enveloped Gifford Ravenscroft's study as the door closed behind Emily. Jacob Stone half smiled at the expressions on the faces of the remaining family members as they stared, speechless, at the door. It was clearly the first time Emily had walked out on her family in the midst of an argument. Possibly the first time anyone had ever walked out on a Ravenscroft during a discussion of any kind.

He felt a surge of fierce, hot pride in Emily. His lady had guts. She had gone through some major changes since he had last seen her. She had come into her own. Those changes might make all the difference now. For the first time, he knew for certain he had been right to return to the States.

It was time at last to claim his woman. Jacob unfolded his arms and moved out of the shadows.

"What the devil has gotten into her?" Gifford fumed. "She's never acted like this before in her life."

Catherine shook her head. "I can't believe she just listened to that tape and then calmly walked out of here."

Drake said nothing but his eyes had a thoughtful expression.

Jacob moved silently toward the door.

"Where are you going, Stone?" Gifford demanded.

"I'm going to drive her back to Seattle." He didn't wait for the stunned reaction to that statement. Jacob opened the door and went through, closing it behind him as quietly as Emily had done a moment earlier.

He strode quickly through the hall and out onto the graceful veranda that surrounded the first level of the house. He was in time. Emily's compact little station wagon was still sitting in the driveway. He loped down the steps and over to the vehicle, reaching it just as Emily leaned forward to twist the key in the ignition. Jacob opened the door.

"I'll drive," he said.

She turned a startled face up to him, her amber eyes widening in the faint light from the veranda. "You'll what?"

"I said I'll drive." He eased in beside her, forcing her gently into the other seat. He had to move swiftly, before she could gather her senses and start thinking. "Fasten your seat belt." It always amazed him how easily people would follow clear orders when they were totally confused and upset. Emily automatically reached for her belt. Jacob was already buckling his own and switching on the engine.

"What do you think you're doing, Mr. Stone?"

"A favor." He wheeled the little car out of the drive, not bothering to glance back at the lighted veranda to see if the rest of the Ravenscrofts were watching. "I'm going to drive you home."

"As my mother pointed out, home is two hundred miles away, and I don't need any more favors from you. You've done enough for me. I'm sure you'll understand if I don't thank you for all your hard work. Stop this car and get out."

But she was sitting stiffly in the seat, her hands in her lap, and Jacob knew now she was not going to try anything foolish such as leaping out of the car. He kept his attention on the rain-slick street that wound down the hillside and spoke calmly.

"You handled them very well this time, Emily. I was proud of you."

"Do you think I care about your opinion?" she asked tightly.

"Probably not." Jacob glanced sideways. She was staring out the windshield, her gentle profile illuminated by the streetlights. Emily was the youngest and definitely the softest of the Ravenscroft clan, but she had the distinctive family features.

Her jet-black hair swung just above her shoulders in a smooth, shining mass. Her wide, amber eyes, framed by soft bangs, were slightly tilted at the outer corners, reminding Jacob of a cat. Her face was fine boned and delicate, like the rest of her. She had an exotic, almost feline grace that she seemed totally unaware of. He rather liked the glasses. Two years ago she had worn contact lenses.

Jacob had found himself fascinated by her tonight as he had watched her from the shadows. Two years had passed since he had last seen her, but he had known the instant she walked into the study that nothing had changed. The old hunger had not died. He still wanted her.

In fact, he acknowledged, as he drove down out of the hills toward the interstate, he wanted her a lot more now than he had two years ago. Tonight he had seen the new womanly strength in her as well as the captivating femininity, and the combination was dynamite. No wonder Morrell was licking his lips and waiting to pounce. All this and a chunk of Ravenscroft International, too. Morrell must have thought he'd landed in clover the day he came across Emily Ravenscroft.

"The tape wasn't faked, Emily," Jacob said into the silence. "That was Morrell talking about his plans to cripple Ravenscroft through you. And that woman he was speaking to was his mistress. A woman named Marcia. I can prove it, if you really have any doubts."

"How did you get the tape?" Emily asked in disgust. "Did you hide under their bed?"

Jacob's mouth hardened. "No. That little scene was not taped in a bedroom. You heard the voice of the waiter and the clatter of dishes. Morrell and the woman met in a restaurant. A place they've been using almost every week for the past year. People tend to be predictable in their daily habits, even nasty people like Morrell."

"That aspect of human nature must greatly simplify your life. You don't have to spend a large amount of time snooping around bedroom windows and garbage cans. You just figure out your victims' habits and take advantage of established routines. Nice work."

He heard the grim anger in her voice and sighed. It wasn't going to be easy. His fingers opened and closed around the steering wheel as he guided the small station wagon onto the interstate and headed toward Seattle. "I know you have a low opinion of my job skills, Emily, but I give you my word I don't make my living snooping around bedroom windows and garbage cans. I never have."

"The little *favor* you did for my family was an exception?"

"You're not going to believe this, but I did it for your sake, not theirs." *Most of all, I did it for my sake,* Jacob added silently. There was no way in hell he could let her marry Morrell now.

"How noble of you." Her eyes raked him as she glanced briefly in his direction. "I assume you were motivated by the same sort of gallantry this time as you were last time? What a lucky woman I am to have a knight hovering in the background who can be relied on to dash in and humiliate me whenever the rest of the Ravenscrofts decide I've made a mistake in my love life."

"Nobody wanted to humiliate you. But you had made a mistake. A big one. Your family was desperate to put a stop to your association with Damon Morrell, and they said you'd ignored all their warnings."

"Just as they were desperate to put a stop to my relationship with Brad Carlton two years ago. At least last time I didn't have to listen to any embarrassing tapes." Emily clenched her hands in her lap. "That was the worst part, you know. Listening to that tape tonight and knowing everyone else in the room had already heard it. I could feel all of you watching me. I knew what you were thinking. Poor, foolish little Emily has been duped again by a man." She paused for a moment and then added quietly, "I don't think I shall ever forgive any of you for the way you did it this time."

Jacob felt his stomach tighten with tension. "Maybe it wasn't well-handled. None of us, your family or myself, are subtle people. We thought a quick, clean approach would be best. You wouldn't have believed me or your parents if there hadn't been proof. That's why I made the tape. I couldn't think of any other way to convince you that Morrell was a lying bastard."

"You mean you didn't think you could simply buy him off the way Dad had you buy off Brad two years ago?"

Jacob swore softly. "Brad Carlton was an ambitious, greedy young man. He thought he could get a head start in life by marrying into your family, but the truth was, he wasn't all that eager to get married. He was more than happy to have the money without taking the vows."

"So my father sent you, his loyal errand boy, to buy him off."

Jacob's temper began to flare. He told himself he was prepared to be tolerant up to a point, but Emily was beginning to push him. He'd never seen her in quite this mood. "When I offered him a lump sum in cash to call off the wedding, he fell all over himself grabbing the money."

"And then the family fell all over me pointing out what a fool I had been. At least I got out tonight before the lecture." Emily looked at him again. "I assume I'm stuck with you all the way to Seattle?"

"Unless you want to turn around and go back to spend the night at your parents' house," he said gently.

"Would you, if you were me?"

Jacob blinked owlishly. "No," he finally admitted. "I probably would have done what you did. Walked out. I told you, I was proud of you."

Emily was silent for a moment. "Were they surprised that I dared to do it?"

"Very surprised."

"Good. It's nice to know I didn't play out the entire scene the way they intended it to be played. I'll take my little consolations where I can. I suppose you're insisting on driving me back to Seattle for my own good, just like you made that tape for my own good?"

Jacob squelched his rising irritation. "Yes."

"Terrific. How are you going to get back to Portland?"

He shrugged. "I can fly back or take the train tomorrow."

She folded her arms under her breasts and leaned back into the corner of the seat. "Where do you plan to spend the night?"

He winced at the soft challenge in her voice. "A hotel, I suppose. I take it you're not going to offer to let me sleep on your couch?"

"Nope. I don't owe you a damned thing, least of all a bed for the night. You're used to taking care of yourself, Jacob. I'm sure you'll be just fine on your own. Tell me something—is it true what my father said? That you quit Ravenscroft International a couple of months ago?"

The question surprised him. He decided to take advantage of the opportunity to tell her about his plans. "It's true. I left Ravenscroft because I've got some ideas of my own for the future. I intend to set up a consulting firm that will cater to companies interested in getting into the overseas construction market. Basically I'll be selling advice. After working for RI for six years, I know the territory."

"I see." She regarded him appraisingly. There was a long pause and then she asked quietly. "You never remarried?"

"No."

Emily heard the short, clipped word and wondered at its meaning. Some of the battle-ready anger in her was fading at last. It took energy to fuel that kind of fury, and she was tired. It had been a long day.

"That's right," she said grimly. "I seem to remember you gave me quite a lecture on the subject of marriage two years ago, right after you told me how quickly Brad Carlton had taken the money you offered."

"I was in the middle of a messy divorce," Jacob said bluntly. "The situation colored my opinion on the institution of marriage."

"I recall you telling me marriage was an idiot's invention. You told me you never intended to marry again and that if I had any sense, I'd never get married at all."

"I told you, I was biased against marriage at the time."

Emily shook her head slightly. "You were so very cynical in those days. I don't imagine much has changed."

Jacob drew a deep breath. "Do you really hate me so much, Emily?"

"Do you care?"

"Yes. I'd like to know exactly how you feel."

"Why?" she demanded.

"Because I want to know how far I'm going to have to go in order to change your mind."

"About you?" She was startled. "Why should it matter to you what I think?"

"If you're honest, you'll admit you already know the answer to that."

"I'm honest enough," she retorted, "but apparently I'm not too bright. I haven't the vaguest idea of what you're talking about or why you care what I think about you."

"Then your family is probably right. You're still very naïve when it comes to men."

"Jacob Stone, what in the world are you trying to say?"

"I'm trying to tell you that I want you," he said roughly. "I've wanted you since I first met you five years ago, but it was always the wrong time and place and I always managed to convince myself I was the wrong man."

Emily was dumbfounded. "You want me? You wanted me five years ago? But that's impossible! Jacob, you never said anything, never implied . . ."

"What did you expect?" he muttered. "In the beginning, you were off-limits because I was married. Then, even when I knew my marriage wasn't going to last, I refused to let myself think I had a right to approach you. You were too young, too soft and gentle. I was too old for you, too battle scarred, and to top it all off I was about to be divorced. Besides, I knew your family would be furious if they realized I wanted you, and I knew you probably wouldn't have been able to take them on for my sake."

Emily sat frozen as she listened to him. Suddenly she could hardly catch her breath. "And after the divorce," she demanded tightly, "why didn't you say anything then?"

"After the divorce I was feeling bitter and disillusioned. I wanted my freedom again but I also wanted you. I was trying to figure out how to approach you when Brad Carlton came on the scene. Without any warning you were announcing your engagement. Your family asked me to get rid of Carlton and I was more than happy to do it. I delighted in doing it. But afterward I knew you hated my guts because I was the one who'd been sent to buy off the jerk. I felt like the guy who takes the little girl's teddy bear away from her and stomps it into the mud.

"I figured I'd get over you," Jacob admitted. "After all, there wasn't much to get over. We hadn't even been to bed together. And I knew you sure as hell weren't pining for me. Your heart was set on Carlton."

"You were right on that point!" Emily was seething again. He would never know that she had taken refuge in Brad's easygoing attentions because she had been so certain there was no hope for a relationship with Jacob. "I don't believe this. You have the nerve to sit there and tell me you'd like to have an affair with me?"

"Yes."

"After what you've done to me?" she demanded disbelievingly.

"I haven't done anything to you. But I've done a couple of very large favors for you. Twice I've saved you from getting married to men who only wanted you because of your connection to Ravenscroft International. One of these days you'll thank me."

Emily was almost speechless. He sounded so sincere. "Don't hold your breath waiting for me to throw myself at your feet in gratitude," she finally snapped.

"I won't." He smiled faintly. The pale glow of the dashboard instruments revealed the underlying grimness of his expression.

"Does my family know about your interest in me?"

"I haven't discussed it with them."

"I'm not surprised. They'd tear you to shreds."

He gave her an odd look. "Not likely. Who would they send to do the job?"

"What?" She was beginning to have a problem following this discussion. It dazed her to think that all this time Jacob might really have wanted her. It wasn't possible. It was some new game he was playing. It had to be.

"You called me an enforcer. Someone paid to intimidate and coerce others," he reminded her.

"Right," she agreed rashly.

"If your family wanted to intimidate or coerce me, who would they get to do it? Who do you send to intimidate a professional intimidator?"

It was too much. Emily began to feel a little light-headed. "I don't think I want to talk about this anymore. This whole evening is beginning to take on a distinct air of unreality. I just want to go home and go to bed."

"I'll see to it," he promised softly.

"You do that." She was silent for a moment and then, frantic to change the subject in order to give herself time to think, she went on. "You said you hadn't worked for Ravenscroft for two months. Why did my family contact you to check out Damon Morrell?"

"Your father and brother knew I was back in the country looking into the possibility of establishing a consulting firm. They contacted me and asked me to do it as a favor. They didn't want to hire an outside investigator if they could avoid it. The fewer people who knew about the situation, the better, as far as they were concerned. They assumed you'd feel more comfortable knowing it was all being kept under close wraps."

"They thought I'd appreciate their thoughtfulness in using you again? They actually thought it would be easier to be humiliated twice by the same man than it would be to be embarrassed by two different investigators?"

"Emily, everyone knew it was going to be hard on you. Give your family credit for trying their best to handle things discreetly."

"What about you? Did you think it would be easier on me knowing you were the messenger boy in both cases?" she asked bitterly.

"Like I said. I did it for your own good."

"Do me a favor, Stone. If you promise not to tell me one more time that you were only involved in this for my own good, I will promise not to strangle you before we get to Seattle."

Jacob smiled his slight, faintly menacing smile. "It's a deal."

2

IT WAS A LONG DRIVE to Seattle. Emily wanted to nap and found it impossible to relax. Her thoughts were churning in the caldron of her mind as she tried to sort out the wholly unexpected twist her life had taken this evening. She had assumed she would probably never see Jacob again. She simply had not been prepared to encounter him tonight. Most of all, she found it difficult to believe that he actually wanted her the way she had been longing for him all these years. It was too much to absorb in one night.

Jacob drove with an expert's smooth touch, but Emily was still uncomfortable. It was his presence in the car, not his driving, that kept her awake. He dominated the small vehicle, filling it with his quiet male power. Emily's only means of retreat was into silence.

When he realized she was not going to respond to his efforts to continue the conversation, Jacob, too, fell silent. It wasn't until he neared the city that he spoke again.

"I have your address. It's downtown somewhere, isn't it? You'd better give me directions," he said.

Emily stirred and told him the route to her apartment building. He followed her instructions without comment. But when he drove the compact into the yawning mouth of the underground garage he glanced around disapprovingly.

"This isn't a good place for you to be arriving alone late at night."

"You sound like my parents and Drake. They came to visit once shortly after I moved in, and all they could talk about was the garage. I'll give you the same answer I gave them. I've survived so far."

She opened the car door as Jacob drove into the parking slot she'd indicated. As she pulled on her coat and retrieved her purse, she acknowledged privately that the garage did seem more than a little forbidding at this hour. Footsteps rang hollowly and the lighting was rather dim. But she was not about to admit the place made her nervous on occasion.

"You can't blame your family for wanting you to be safe," Jacob said as he climbed out of the car.

"My family has tried to protect me since the day I was born. It gets a little wearing at times."

"Sometimes you need protection. You've always had a talent for getting yourself into trouble." Jacob walked beside her toward the elevators. "Take this situation with Damon Morrell, for example."

"Stop worrying about Damon Morrell." Emily stabbed the elevator call button and then shoved her hands into the pockets of her green wool coat.

"When are you going to tell him you won't be seeing him again?" Jacob asked calmly as the elevator doors slid open.

Emily raised her eyebrows above the black frames of her glasses and asked smoothly, "Who says I'm not going to be seeing Damon again?" She was proud of the easy way that came out.

Jacob surveyed her with a cool-eyed gaze. "Don't play games, Emily. You're a little too innocent and naïve for your own good at times, but you're no fool. You know that what you heard on that tape tonight wasn't faked.

Nor was any of the other evidence your family produced."

"You mean the evidence *you* produced at their request. Why should I trust you, Jacob? Give me one good reason."

"You may not like me very much, Emily, but I think you know I wouldn't manufacture a pack of lies."

She eyed his stark features, vibrantly aware of the cold pride in his voice. "I don't know you very well at all, Jacob. At one time I thought I did, but that was a long while ago. Back in my innocent and naïve days."

"You should know your own family well enough to know they wouldn't resort to lies. They may not be very subtle at times, but they're honest. And they wouldn't have asked my help if they didn't think they could trust me. Stop looking for excuses." His expression softened slightly. "And stop pretending you don't trust me. You know damned well I'd never do anything to hurt you."

"Unless, of course, it was necessary for my own good," Emily retorted smartly as she stepped off the elevator and into the gray-carpeted hall. She reached into her purse for her keys.

"Emily, I know you've had an upsetting evening, but that's no reason to act like this. Face facts and admit you got hoodwinked by Morrell."

Emily turned the key in the lock, pushed open the door and then turned to confront him from the safety of her own threshold. "It wasn't Damon who misled me, Jacob. It was my honest, well-intentioned, overprotective family. They're the ones who invited me down to Portland for the weekend for what I thought was supposed to be a business discussion about some plans I'm making. They're the ones who hoodwinked me. With your assistance, of course. But you've always been available when they needed help in saving me from myself, haven't you? Good night, Jacob. I won't say it was a pleasure seeing you again after all this time, but I'll admit it was something of a surprise."

"Emily, that wasn't the way it happened." Jacob caught the edge of the door as she tried to close it in his face. "Listen to me. No one lied to you. If you'd stuck around, you could have had the business discussion you wanted. But everyone felt it was best to get the matter of your relationship with Morrell out of the way first. Be reasonable. We only did it for your own—"

"Don't say it," she warned. "Don't you dare say it was for my own good. If I hear that one more time I won't be responsible for what happens, Jacob."

"Stop threatening me or I might be tempted to do something rash myself." Jacob sounded totally exasperated.

Emily could not resist taunting him. She had had enough for one evening, and Jacob was the logical target of her hostility. For five long years he had, in one way or another, been the object of too many of her strongest emotions. No reason that should change now. "Such as, Mr. Stone?"

He thrust open the door and reached for her without any warning. His hands closed around her shoulders and he pulled her close. "Such as this," he muttered thickly and covered her mouth with his own.

Emily was too startled to offer any resistance at first. Whatever she had been expecting, she told herself, it wasn't this. Or was it? The tension between herself and Jacob had been sizzling just under the surface since she had first walked into the study in her parents' home and seen him waiting in the shadows.

She silently admitted that she had been far more shaken by seeing Jacob Stone again after two years than she had been by the news of Damon Morrell's duplicity.

She made a small sound as he took her mouth, but whatever it was she was trying to say, and she wasn't too sure herself just what that was, it was lost in the intimate embrace. Jacob's mouth was warm and heavy and seductively demanding against her own. This was only the second time he had ever kissed her, and Emily knew now she had been quietly starving for him.

He kissed her as if he had been anticipating the prospect for a long, long time. There was a barely leashed hunger in him that told its own tale.

It was that hunger that made the biggest impact on Emily. It was the masculine version of her own long-suppressed desire, and it overwhelmed her. She had never experienced anything quite like it. She knew then that whatever else might be true about Jacob, one thing was certain. He had said he wanted her, and now, at last, as his kiss seared through her, she believed him.

"Say my name." Jacob's mouth slid tantalizingly over Emily's lips. Gently he outlined her full lower lip with the tip of his tongue until she gasped and parted her lips for him. "Say it, Emily. It's been so long since I've heard you whisper it the way you did that last night two years ago."

"Jacob." His name was a soft sigh of uncertainty and excitement and longing that had been pent up far too long. "Oh, Jacob."

"You've got a voice like raw silk. I've never forgotten it." Jacob lifted his head slightly so that his mouth hovered barely an inch above hers. He looked down into her bemused face and drew a slow, sensual finger along the delicate line of her jaw. "If I had taken you two years ago instead of trying to be so damned gallant, maybe everything would be different now."

"What would have been different?"

"You would already belong to me. We wouldn't have to waste any more time going through the rituals."

"What rituals?" Emily searched his cool gray eyes.

"The ones designed to bring you and me together. Emily, I walked away last time because I thought I was all wrong for you."

"Nothing's changed," she pointed out breathlessly. "You're still just as tough and ruthless and cynical as you always were."

Jacob's mouth tilted slightly at the corner. "I might not have changed, but you have. And that, I think, is going to make all the difference."

"What makes you think I've changed?"

His mouth curved faintly. "I saw you in action tonight when your father delivered the news about Morrell. There's a new strength in you that wasn't there two years ago."

"Assertiveness training," she announced proudly. "I took some classes."

Jacob's eyes reflected his amusement. "I think it's more likely you've finally come into your own. Seeing you now after all this time makes me realize that I was wrong when I thought you needed someone softer and more easygoing than me. You need someone as strong or stronger than you are."

"If I'm so tough and strong, then it follows that I no longer need you or anyone else trying to run my life for me," Emily parried.

Jacob grinned. "You may be a lot stronger than you once were, but that doesn't mean you aren't still a little naïve. Parts of you may have changed, Emily, but not everything. Not the basics. You're still very soft and sweet under that new veneer. The fact that someone like Morrell could come so close to using you proves that when it comes to judging people you're still innocent in a lot of ways. It's nothing to be ashamed of."

"Good, because I'm not feeling particularly ashamed." That was a lie. She was furious with herself for having been fool enough to get involved with Damon Morrell on even a limited basis. But she was not about to admit that to this man or to her family.

"Emily..."

"I think it's time you left. Good luck finding a hotel." She stepped out from under his hands and tried once more to force the door closed.

"I'll need to use your phone to make a reservation and call a cab," Jacob said calmly. He was already moving through the door and into her living room.

Emily gave an exclamation of disgust and stalked into the living room behind him. Imperiously she pointed toward the red phone that was sitting on a white lacquer table near the window. "There's the phone. Call. I'd like you out of here as soon as possible. It's quite late and I need my sleep."

He looked up as he dialed a number out of the phone book. "I'll be on my way as soon as possible. Wouldn't want to overstay my welcome."

"You've already done that."

"But just so you'll be prepared, I should warn you I'll be back soon."

"Without an invitation?"

He lifted one shoulder negligently. "With or without. I think you're going to need a little protection for a while. I promised your family I'd look after you."

"Protection!"

But he wasn't paying her any attention. He was too busy conversing with a hotel registration desk. Emily folded her arms and glared at him. He looked very solid and disconcertingly masculine standing in the middle of her white-on-white living room.

It was a room she had poured a great deal of time and attention into creating. On the surface it was very modern and very sophisticated with its white carpet, white leather couch, glass-and-white lacquer tables and white leather-and-chrome chairs. But there was color everywhere, in the endless bouquets of flowers that filled the place, and the natural beauty of the exquisite blooms made a mockery of the superficial sophistication of the apartment. It was a home that was completely different from the old-fashioned elegance of her parents' house.

Jacob finished his conversation with the hotel and then he called a cab. When he finally set down the receiver again, Emily was waiting to pounce.

"What did you mean by that crack about my needing protection?"

He stood with his feet slightly braced, regarding her with a speculative gaze. "Morrell is not going to be pleased when you tell him you won't be seeing him anymore. He won't like having his plans changed so drastically by a woman he thinks he's got in the palm of his hand. He'll probably assume he can change your mind by putting pressure on you. You're a tempting little fish, and he's not going to let you off the hook easily. He's liable to become difficult."

"He might or might not become difficult if I decided not to see him again. You, on the other hand, already are being difficult. If I have to choose, I'll take Damon's brand of being awkward, whatever that turns out to be. Basically he's a gentleman. I'm sure I'll be able to handle him. That's assuming I decide to end the relationship in the first place."

"You'll end it," Jacob said gently. "You're angry about the way your family and I handled the news this evening, but in the end you'll do what's best. Just do it quickly, Emily. The longer you put it off, the more difficult it's going to be. You heard what your father said earlier. Ravenscroft is preparing a bid against Morrell's firm on the Fowler project down in Dallas. Morrell wants that job. It wouldn't surprise me if he's got plans to keep tabs on Ravenscroft's position through you."

"Now you're really clutching at straws," Emily scoffed. "Damon knows I have almost no idea what Ravenscroft International does on a day-to-day basis. I wouldn't be of much use to him as an industrial spy, even if I wanted to help him land that Dallas job. Stop trying to create monsters where there aren't any. I'm no longer a silly little fool who can be kept in line by dire warnings or heavy-handed guilt trips."

"I keep forgetting your assertiveness training," Jacob said dryly. "Did you graduate with honors?"

"Let's just say I learned a lot."

"I'll bet your instructor didn't teach you anything about handling a man like Morrell."

"I suppose it hasn't occurred to you or my family that I might enjoy having a casual association with a man like Damon? That I might not be planning on marrying him?"

"He's planning on marrying you. That's the problem. You heard the tape. Better to end it fast, Emily. The man's a user and he'll use you. He's out of your league."

"Obviously your opinion of my ability to take care of myself isn't any higher than it was the last time we met, in spite of what you said earlier." Emily held open the door. "Good night, Jacob."

He did not move for a moment, just stood there studying her as if trying to come to some internal conclusions. Emily was seriously beginning to wonder what she would do if he did not leave when he finally broke the impasse and walked toward the door.

"You have turned into one stubborn little cat, Emily Ravenscroft," he observed with a fleeting expression that might have been humor. With Jacob Stone it wasn't always easy to tell.

"The word is 'assertive.' I keep telling you, I've had classes in the subject. I started taking them two years ago when I finally pulled myself up by the bootstraps and decided I was tired of letting my family run my life."

"What are you doing with your life these days?" Jacob asked with a thoughtful frown. "Your mother said something about working in a florist's shop."

"Which is one step above being a scullery maid in her estimation." Emily smiled breezily. "A total waste of a fine liberal arts education and good social background, according to her. But you know what?"

"What?" He looked wary of the answer.

"I love it. I own that shop, and soon, with or without the financial backing of my family, I'm going to open another branch. Who knows? Maybe Damon Morrell will offer to make me the loan I was planning to ask my father for. I can always use my connection to Ravenscroft International as collateral."

Halfway toward the door, Jacob swung around in astonishment. There was a thunderous look on his stark face. "You little cat, you wouldn't dare! Your whole family would hit the roof."

"An interesting thought," she said sweetly. She gave him a firm push that, surprisingly enough, got him over the threshold. "For the last time, good night, Jacob." This time she succeeded in closing the door and locking it behind him.

Outside in the empty hall, Jacob stood glaring at the paneled door. The fluffy little kitten had turned into a tigress with very sharp claws. Amazing how a woman could change in two years. Obviously her family was badly underestimating her.

But somehow, Jacob Stone was finding Emily more interesting than ever.

His chief victory for the evening, he decided as he stepped into the elevator, was a minor one, but under the circumstances he would take what he could get.

She had kissed him with all the passion she had shown two years ago and more. She still wanted him.

Jacob savored that simple fact as he walked out into the damp night.

EMILY HAD STOPPED SEETHING by the time she opened Emily's Garden early the next morning, but she was still aware of a lingering residue of humiliation and dismay. She did not plan to admit it to her family or to Jacob, but the unfortunate truth was that Damon Morrell had completely fooled her. She had never once guessed that he was interested in her because of her relationship to Ravenscroft International.

The only thing she could say in her favor was that she had never planned on marrying the man. As far as Emily was concerned, he was a pleasant companion and an interesting and amusing date. That was all. Not one of her family or Jacob had bothered to inquire as to how serious she actually was about Damon, of course. With typical Ravenscroft-Stone arrogance, they had all assumed the worst. They had also assumed that she was nothing but a helpless pawn of Morrell's.

Emily sighed as she arranged fresh yellow tulips and chrysanthemums in the front window of the shop. The embarrassing truth was that if she had been serious about Morrell, she might, indeed, have found herself in a real disaster of a situation.

It was infuriating to realize that after all her efforts to stand on her own two feet and resist the intrusiveness of her family, she could have come so close to making such a major mistake.

Not that the Ravenscrofts would ever have allowed her to actually marry Morrell, Emily thought wryly. Somehow or other, her family would have found a way to put a stop to such a plan, just as a way had been found to get rid of Brad Carlton two years ago. It was highly doubtful that any man who did not fit the Ravenscroft image of a perfect son-in-law would be allowed to marry her. And Emily did not, offhand, know of any man who would have the courage to marry her if her family decided to object. Ravenscrofts could be very persuasive.

And when persuasion did not work, her family sent in the heavy artillery: Jacob Stone.

The memory of Jacob's kiss intruded at that moment, and Emily's fingers tightened around the delicate stems of the tulips. For a moment she stared out the shop window at the sidewalk full of people on their way downtown to shop in the rain. One thought filled her mind. Jacob wanted her.

The door opened and Diane Ames, Emily's assistant, sauntered in, dripping cheerfully. She was a couple of years younger than Emily and tended toward the slightly outrageous in clothing and hairstyles, but she was an intelligent young woman with a genuine flair for flowers and design. Emily considered her a prize and often told herself that her judgment of human nature could not be totally faulty or she would never have had the sense to hire Diane.

"What in the world are you doing here?" Diane demanded as she set a Styrofoam cup of coffee on the counter and shook out her umbrella. "It's Saturday. I thought you were spending the weekend in sunny Portland." She shrugged out of the shiny taxi-yellow rain slicker she was wearing.

"Portland wasn't very sunny, after all."

Diane peered at her from eyes that were outlined by vivid makeup. "Uh-oh, what happened? The family wasn't interested in loaning you the money to open the new shop on Fourth?"

"The subject never came up," Emily explained grimly as she went behind the counter to open the cash register for the day. "My family had something else on their collective brain."

"Something else?" Diane hung up the raincoat and reached for her coffee. "Like what?"

"Like my love life."

Diane choked on her first sip. "Your *what*?"

"You heard me." Emily glared at her assistant's overdone expression of astonishment and grinned in spite of her bad mood. "I know. What love life? You don't have to look so stunned. I do have the occasional date now and then."

Diane looked dubious. "The only man you've been dating recently is that good-looking Damon Morrell, and I recall you telling me distinctly he was just a 'friend.'"

"My family thought it might amount to more than that."

"So? Where's the problem if it did? Morrell's got everything most mothers would kill for in a son-in-law. He's making a fortune in that construction company he inherited from his father, he knows how to dress for success and he works out four times a week at a health club. What more could a parent ask?"

"They would prefer that he did not happen to own a company that's in direct competition with Ravenscroft International," Emily said succinctly. "You have to understand that where my family is concerned, business always comes first. They assume everyone else operates under the same premise. They, therefore, came to the conclusion that there's only one reason Damon Morrell might be seeing me on a regular basis."

Diane stared at her and then realization dawned in her blue eyes. "Good grief, you don't mean they're afraid he's got his eyes on you because of your position at RI?"

"Bingo," Emily said with mock approval. "Go to the head of the class."

"And that's what they wanted to talk to you about this weekend?"

"They invited me down for the weekend to talk business," Emily said. "I, of course, naïvely assumed they meant they were finally willing to listen to my proposal about a loan for the new shop. As you can imagine, there was a slight communication problem."

"Oh, Emily, how awful. What did they say? How did they handle it?"

"They handled it the way they often handle a crisis. They called in Jacob Stone."

"You're losing me," Diane warned. "Who's Jacob Stone?"

Emily drummed her fingers on the counter, considering that question. "Jacob has worked for my family for several years, although I'm told he officially resigned from RI a couple of months ago. Obviously he didn't really sever his ties with the firm or he wouldn't have been available for checking out Damon Morrell."

"What was his position with Ravenscroft?"

"His position?" Emily narrowed her eyes. "Officially he was a vice president in charge of certain aspects of overseas construction operations. But unofficially he was my family's personal troubleshooter. When the going got tough, my family's motto was Send Stone. Problems on the construction site? Labor difficulties? Industrial espionage? Trouble with local laws? Send Stone. One hundred percent reliable. Totally discreet. Utterly loyal. Always gets the job done with a minimum of fuss. In short, the perfect employee. I always thought of him as a paid enforcer. If my family had been a bunch of hoods instead of reasonably respectable business people, Jacob probably would have been a hit man."

"He sounds fascinating." Diane took another sip of coffee. "So your family called him back into temporary service when they wanted Damon vetted, huh?"

"Right. It's not the first time they've used him to get me out of what they considered trouble."

"When was the first time?" Diana asked.

Emily arched one brow behind her glasses, remembering. "The first time I ever encountered Jacob was five years ago. He had joined the company a year before that, but I hadn't run into him. No reason why I should have. RI is a big firm, and I rarely met many of the employees."

"So how did you happen to meet him when you did?"

Emily sighed. "I got myself kidnapped."

"Good God! You're joking?"

"Afraid not. A deranged employee who had recently been let go by RI decided to grab me and hold me for ransom. He somehow tracked me down at college and cornered me one night as I was walking back from the library. He had a gun."

Diane looked severely shaken. "How awful."

Emily made a face. "It sounds worse than it was. Oh, I was scared to death at first, but then I realized the man was more to be pitied than feared. He would never have used the gun. In fact, I later found out it was empty. But it looked real enough at the time, so I did what he said. He drove me to a cabin he had in the woods and started making ransom calls to my folks."

"How did Jacob get involved?"

"My parents called in Jacob and asked him to handle the payoff. They wanted someone they could trust completely. They didn't want the police involved at that point. They were terrified I'd get killed. Jacob talked to the man on the phone who gave him instructions where to deliver the money. Then I was allowed to talk to Jacob myself. Fortunately the guy holding me was half panicked and not thinking very straight. I managed to give Jacob enough clues that he was able to figure out where I was being held."

"So Jacob showed up with the payoff and you were set free?"

"Not exactly," Emily said. "Jacob located the cabin and came in through a back window. The guy who had grabbed me never knew what hit him."

Diane's eyes were very wide. "Jacob rescued you! How incredibly romantic."

"Not really. As far as everyone was concerned, it was just one more dumb mess I'd gotten myself into. Even Jacob yelled at me for being so stupid as to walk back through the campus alone at night and expose myself to risk. I was mortified and humiliated, as usual." And she had fallen madly in love with her rescuer, only to discover that Jacob Stone was married. At the time it had seemed like the end of the world.

"It's not unusual for people to yell at someone who's just given them a major fright. Parents yell at kids all the time for just that reason. Out of curiosity, what was the outcome of the investigation involving Damon Morrell? Or did your Mr. Stone find out anything really interesting other than the fact that Morrell's a competitor with RI?"

Emily paused and then decided there was no reason to be coy. "Jacob Stone could find something incriminating about an angel if someone assigned him the task."

Diane leaned on the counter, her coffee cup cradled in both hands. "Okay, let's have it. What did he find out about Damon?"

"It's embarrassing, Diane."

"That's what friends are for."

Emily's mouth curved. "To embarrass myself in front of?"

"Come on. We have no secrets from each other. If you can't tell me, who can you tell?"

"You may be right." Emily sighed. "Jacob turned up evidence that Damon Morrell intended to marry me in order to gain control of my shares in Ravenscroft International."

"Evidence? Stone found actual proof? How?"

"There was a nasty little tape recording he made at a restaurant. On it is a conversation between Damon and a woman named Marcia."

"Who's Marcia?"

"Damon's mistress, apparently. He took her to lunch and explained to her that she wasn't to be jealous of what he was planning to do. He intended to marry me long enough to gain control of my RI shares and then he intended to get divorced and marry Marcia. In addition to the tape, there were also a couple of incriminating memos Damon sent a couple of years ago vowing vengeance on Ravenscroft, regardless of what it took or what it cost. Apparently his dislike of RI goes beyond the normal feelings of a competitor. He hates my family and the firm."

Diane's mouth fell open. "How strange. Why does he hate Ravenscroft?"

"I don't know. Something to do with a bid Morrell lost a couple of years ago. My father and brother didn't want to burden me with the whole sordid tale, naturally. They consider me very naïve when it comes to the harsh realities of big business. All they're concerned about is making sure I don't marry Damon."

"Did you tell them you hadn't planned to marry him?"

Emily smiled, the first smile reflecting genuine humor since she had walked into her father's study. "Are you kidding? I had to salvage something from the fiasco. I decided not to give any of them, including Jacob Stone, the satisfaction of knowing they didn't have to worry about me marrying Damon. Let them stew about it for a while. I'm sick and tired of them interfering in my life."

The phone on the counter rang just as Diane opened her mouth to demand more answers. Emily picked up the receiver.

"Emily's Garden."

"There you are, dear. I tried your apartment, but you'd already left."

"Hello, Mom," Emily said crisply. "I'm a little busy. What can I do for you?"

"I just wanted to make sure you were all right and that everything had been taken care of," Catherine Ravenscroft said soothingly. "Your father and I were a little worried about you. You seemed so upset when you left last night."

"Upset? Did I seem upset? I can't imagine how you got that impression. Why should I have been upset?" Emily kept her voice artificially light and taunting. She could visualize her mother's frown on the other end of the line.

"Now, Emily, you know we only want what's best for you. You were on the verge of making a terrible mistake. Just as you did that time you got involved with Carlton. Come to think of it, you've never really shown good judgment when it comes to men. I remember that boy with the motorcycle back when you were in high school . . ."

"Bobby Hadley? Give me a break, Mom. Bobby was a decent kid. Besides, I was interested in his bike, not him. You never gave him a chance. You wouldn't even let him in the house, much less let me go out with him."

"How did we get off on the subject of Bobby Hadley?" her mother wanted to know. "I was talking about Morrell. You must understand, dear, that we simply couldn't allow you to get any more involved with Damon Morrell. I hope Jacob had a nice long talk with you on the drive back to Seattle last night. He's always so good at making people see reason."

"I hate to tell you this, but I dozed most of the way. Jacob's a good driver. Since I didn't have to worry about watching the road, I napped."

"Emily, what's the matter with you? You've become increasingly stubborn and difficult during the past couple of years. Ever since your grandmother died and you opened that shop, you've been changing. I don't know what's gotten into you."

"Maybe the problem is that I'm no longer a little girl, Mom."

"I will assume that you've still got enough sense to be reasonable about this situation with Damon Morrell," Catherine said frostily. "I will also assume that you will be attending your father's birthday party in two weeks."

"That's a big assumption."

"Emily!"

"Oh, stop worrying. Of course I'll be at the party. I wouldn't want you to send Jacob Stone out to collect me, would I?"

"I don't know what you have against Jacob. He's always been such a good, reliable employee," Catherine said in exasperation. "So loyal. We were very sorry to lose him two months ago. Drake will certainly miss him. He had come to rely on him just as Giff had."

"I'm sure Drake will find a replacement," Emily said without a lot of concern.

"Never mind. About your father's birthday party. It will be formal, as always."

"You mean I can't show up in jeans?"

"Lately your sense of humor has become very strange, Emily. Goodbye, dear. See you in a couple of weeks." Catherine's motherly instincts kicked in somewhat belatedly. "And don't waste your energy pining over Damon Morrell. He certainly isn't worth any tears."

"I'll keep that in mind," Emily said dryly. She replaced the receiver with an annoyed crash.

"Well?" Diane asked chattily as she began arranging flowers in the display refrigerator. "What did Mom want?"

"She was just checking to make sure I had been properly brought to heel last night at the family conference."

Diane arched her brows. "And have you?"

"Well, I've certainly lost what little interest I had in Damon, but I'll be darned if I'll let Jacob or the family know that, at least not for a while. Won't do them any harm to sweat it out a bit."

Diane peered at her through a twisting mass of greenery. "You are annoyed with that bunch, aren't you?"

"Very." Emily paused. "But maybe not so much with Jacob as I am with my family."

"Why not? Seems to me he did the dirty work this time around."

Emily made a face. "He always does the dirty work. He's good at it. But part of me feels sort of sympathetic."

"Sympathetic!"

"I know. It's hard to explain. It's just that, deep down, he's a decent man and he's always acted out of loyalty to my family and to the firm. He really did believe he was acting in my best interests this time around."

"You're making excuses for him, Emily. Why?"

"How should I know?" Emily admitted with a groan. "Maybe it's because I've never forgotten the way I felt five years ago when I was sitting in that cabin with that maniac and Jacob Stone came through the window. You can find a lot of excuses for a man who once came to your rescue in a big way."

"Yeah," agreed Diane thoughtfully. "You can."

3

ON MONDAY MORNING Emily was in the middle of experimenting with a deceptively simple design using three magnificent daisies and a spray of myrtle when she again allowed herself to think about Jacob Stone. She had been thinking about him on and off since Saturday. The truth was, she couldn't get him out of her mind. There was no getting around the fact that she was secretly disappointed he hadn't reappeared on Sunday.

She also wondered what her father would say if he knew that his handpicked troubleshooter was not only happy to save Emily from a dangerous marriage, he was also interested in taking her to bed.

Gifford Ravenscroft would be outraged. Catherine Ravenscroft would be livid. And as for Drake, well, Drake was a little less predictable, but Emily was almost certain he wouldn't approve. He was as protective of Emily as everyone else in the family.

Emily knew her family well enough to guess that although they might be willing to use Jacob Stone's peculiar talents when it suited them, they were not likely to view him as any more suitable as a son-in-law than they had Brad Carlton or Damon Morrell.

The Ravenscrofts were not above trying to arrange a marriage for their one and only daughter. As with most other things in life, Emily's family tended to view marriage as a business matter. Emily had been introduced to enough "suitable" men by her parents to know exactly what type they had in mind for her. Someone established and successful in his own right, with good family and social connections. Someone who would be willing to sign a contract guaranteeing he would keep his hands off Emily's shares in Ravenscroft International.

Emily grinned as she thought of the shares she owned. They definitely constituted a thorn in the side of the rest of the Ravenscrofts. But Grandmother Emelina Ravenscroft had always been good at irritating the other Ravenscrofts. She had always considered herself their conscience. It had been her money that had originally started Ravenscroft International, although she freely admitted it had been her husband's natural predatory qualities that had made the firm so successful. It had been the perfect marriage combining money and business talent and RI had prospered.

Emily's grandfather had left his shares of the firm to his son, Gifford, and his grandson, Drake. But her grandmother had stunned everyone by leaving her piece of the firm to Emily. No one had quite recovered from the shock.

When the family had gathered itself sufficiently to think logically once more, Emily had been told that it would be best if she surrendered her interest to her father and brother. The firm could not afford to buy her out.

Emily, remembering the deathbed promise she had made in private to her grandmother, had calmly refused. She had never explained what had been said between herself and her grandmother during that private interview, and no one had thought to ask. All the rest of the family cared about was the fact that for the first time in her life, Emily was defying them.

It had been her first major act of defiance, and no one had believed she would stand firm. It was assumed she would give in on this matter just as she had crumpled at the age of eighteen when she had been informed she would go to an exclusive private college, not join an artists' colony as she had planned.

Two years had passed since Emily had started Emily's Garden against her family's wishes, but the Ravenscrofts still had trouble believing Emily had truly changed.

"Practicing for the big flower show, Emily?" Diane asked casually as she came through the shop door after lunch. She peered at the delicate design taking shape under Emily's fingers. "I like that arrangement, but frankly I've got to tell you it might be a little too subtle for the judges. You know how they were last year."

"Just because I didn't win last year doesn't mean the judges don't respect subtlety," Emily said. "We have to take into account the possibility that the winning entry was actually a better design than the one I submitted."

"Hah. I refuse to admit that." Diane made a theatrical gesture with her right hand. "Yours was perfect. Magnificent. A tribute to the melding of two cultures. You combined the Japanese approach to celebrating the harmony and grandeur in nature with the Western love of opulence. It was a work of art and the judges were blind. This year, skip the simple celebration of harmony and grandeur and go for opulence."

Emily frowned consideringly down at her creation. "You think so?"

"Trust me. Give 'em glitz and dazzle this year. You've got to hit those turkey judges over the head with color and lushness. We're dealing with simple brains that need to be stimulated by glitter. They're incapable of appreciating the subtle approach."

"Speaking of simple brains," Emily interrupted, remembering a business matter. "The secretary from Baker, Schmidt and Baker called just after you went out to lunch."

"Just because Baker, Schmidt and Baker are a bunch of advertising executives doesn't mean they're all simple-minded, Emily."

"I suppose you're right. I shouldn't jump to conclusions. At any rate, the firm is giving a reception for its clients on the fifth next month, and they want us to do the flowers."

"Great. We'll have to notify the wholesalers by the end of this week if we want to be sure they'll have everything we need in stock."

"I know. We'd better put a list together today. By the way—"

Emily broke off as the phone rang. Automatically she reached out to pick up the receiver. Too late she realized she should have let Diane answer it. Damon Morrell's deep voice came on the line. Damon had a way of making the most mundane greeting sound surprisingly intimate.

"Hey, how's my favorite flower lady today? How was the trip to Portland?" Damon asked with characteristic easy confidence. "I missed you, Emily. Spent a very dull weekend. I hope yours was equally dull. I thought we might we able to squeeze in dinner tomorrow night. What do you say?"

Emily hesitated, wishing she'd had her excuses ready. "I'm afraid I'm going to be busy tomorrow night, Damon." Weak. Very weak.

"I'm adaptable. How about doing something this evening? I just got back from a raquetball game and I'm about to step into a shower. What do you say I pick you up around seven? We'll have dinner at that little Italian café in the market."

It was his automatic assumption that she would be available on such short notice that made Emily realize just how close Damon had been getting lately. She had thought of him as a casual, friendly companion for the past few weeks, but suddenly she had to acknowledge that he might have been stalking her. Without her being really aware of it, the relationship had somehow gotten to the point where Damon fully expected her to accept any invitation he extended. She wondered if he was going to break a date with the mysterious Marcia in order to be free tonight.

It was time to start easing out of the situation. Preferably without any major confrontations. Emily hated confrontations. She was much better at handling them than she used to be, thanks to her assertiveness training course, but she still disliked the emotional turmoil they caused within her. Too many years of trying to appease her family had taken its toll.

"Thanks, Damon, but I've already made plans for this evening and I'm sure you have, too. Maybe some other time."

There was a startled moment of silence on the other end of the line. Then Damon said lightly. "Other plans? Me? Are you kidding? No such luck. I was just going to have a sandwich and go over a few papers at home." His voice became coaxing. "Come on, honey, let's get together tonight. We can try another place if you don't want Italian food. I'm open and I really want to see you. Name your poison."

Emily summoned up her assertiveness training. "Thank you for the invitation, Damon, but I'm afraid I'm not free tonight."

"Well, if you don't feel like going out, we can eat in. I'll pick up some takeout from a delicatessen and a bottle of wine and we can relax at your place."

There was an underlying forcefulness in Damon's voice now. He was a man who was accustomed to getting his own way. It occurred to Emily that she knew entirely too many people who had that problem. She closed her eyes and repeated the simple, nonconfrontational words just as she had been taught. Quiet repetition was the trick.

"Thank you for the invitation, Damon, but I'm afraid I'm not free tonight."

"How about Wednesday night?" he demanded instantly.

Emily swallowed. "I'm going to be busy Wednesday night, also."

"Is that right?" Damon sounded distinctly skeptical. "Well, maybe early next week. I'll give you a call. Have a good time tonight and tomorrow night and Wednesday." He hung up the phone with a cool impatience that filtered through the line.

Emily shuddered with relief as she replaced the receiver. Diane was watching her.

"That was Damon Morrell getting the brush-off?"

"I'm afraid so. All I could think about was that tape recording of him telling his lady friend that he was going to marry me in order to get control of my RI shares. Somehow the magic went out of the relationship after I heard that."

"I can see why. I must say you handled it well. Very calm and nonconfrontational."

"My assertiveness instructor would be proud," Emily agreed dryly.

"Of course, that leaves you with an empty evening," Diane pointed out.

"It won't be the first. I'll do something exciting like wash my hair. Hand me that bunch of snapdragons, will you? And that lily. You may be right—this might be the year to go for glitz and glamour."

"Now you're talking."

But at five o'clock that afternoon, Emily glanced up from putting the last of the unsold flowers into the cooler and got the distinct impression she was not going to be spending the evening alone washing her hair, after all.

Jacob Stone walked purposefully through the front door, and Emily instantly conjured up images of bulls in china shops. He came to a halt in the middle of the small store, and Emily changed her mind. He wasn't exactly a bull tiptoeing through stacks of delicate china cups and saucers. He was more like a dragon in a tea garden.

Jacob paused and looked around with considerable interest. He was wearing a gray windbreaker over a dark shirt and dark trousers. He had made no concession to the light mist that was falling outside and his hair was damp. He took his time examining the place as if mentally cataloging every square inch of it.

"Can I help you?" Diane asked cheerfully. Her eyes were speculative as she ran them over the newcomer.

Jacob spared her a short glance and then his gaze moved on to Emily, who was watching him from behind a huge bunch of yellow jonquils.

"No, thanks. I came to ask Emily to have dinner with me. Hello, Emily."

Emily peered at him through the flowers. "Hello, Jacob. This is a surprise."

"Isn't it, though?" Diane said without batting an eye. "And an interesting one, too. Emily has other plans for the evening. She's going to wash her hair. So you're Jacob?"

Jacob switched his gaze back to her. "That's right. Jacob Stone."

"Ah, yes," Diane said wisely. "You're the one who periodically steps in to rescue Emily. I heard all about the way you tracked down the guy who was holding her for ransom five years ago."

"Is that right?" Jacob studied Diane more closely, and then he smiled his cryptic smile. "Did she tell you that when I came through the window all set to deal with a crazed maniac wielding a gun I found Emily playing gin rummy with her kidnapper? He had put the gun down on a table and Emily was keeping score. Everything was so calm and ordinary that I thought I'd broken into the wrong cabin."

"No," Diane murmured with great interest, "she didn't tell me that part. But Emily has a way of charming the strangest people. Who won the gin game?"

"It wasn't funny," Emily said reproachfully. "I felt very sorry for that poor man. He was mentally ill, but he never really meant any harm. He was just feeling alone and desperate."

Jacob shook his head. "Amazing, isn't it?" he said to Diane. "The guy kidnaps her at gunpoint, holds her for nearly forty-eight hours and then she says she felt sorry for him."

"Well, I did feel sorry for him," Emily muttered. "But the main reason I started the gin game was to get him to put down the gun. I was getting nervous having it pointed at me all the time."

"I can imagine," Diane said, shaking her head with the same disbelieving air Jacob had used. "You're right, Mr. Stone. It is amazing. Good night, you two." She picked up her purse and headed for the door. "Hope you both have a great time playing in the soap suds. See you, Emily." She was out the door before Emily could think of an excuse to get her to stay. The shop seemed very quiet after she left.

"I thought you'd be back in Portland by now," Emily said as she put the jonquils in the cooler.

"I flew back Saturday morning, picked up some things and drove back to Seattle today." He was watching her intently.

"Just to make sure I follow orders regarding Damon Morrell? You really do go above and beyond the call of duty, don't you?"

"I came back to see you, Emily," he said steadily.

"Did you?" She realized the strange feeling she felt inside herself was from some new and alien form of excitement. It was as if she had been anticipating Jacob's arrival all day, which was patently ridiculous. Desperately she tried to calm herself.

"I had to take care of the Morrell situation for your family first, Emily. Then I thought I'd give you a day or so to put things back into perspective. Do you understand about Morrell?"

She thought of what it must be like as a trusted employee to receive a direct request from the boss. What else could Jacob have done except agree to handle Morrell, she wondered. "Yes, I understand."

He nodded, clearly relieved at her unexpectedly reasonable attitude. "I knew you would once you'd had a chance to think about it. Your relationship with him was dangerous for you. But that's all behind us now." He hesitated and then said bluntly, "I'd like to take you to dinner tonight."

"Jacob, I—"

He cut her off quickly, his brows forming a heavy, intent line. "I know you're probably still a little upset with me for my part in that business with Morrell, but you're an intelligent woman, Emily. You know I only did what I had to do. So did your family, for that matter. Let me take you to dinner." He smiled bleakly. "I owe you that much, at least."

Emily scowled at him, not liking the way he had phrased that last part. It reminded her too much of his situation with her family. "I suppose you're the kind who always pays his debts?"

He gave her an odd look. "Sure."

"How unfortunate for you," Emily said, being deliberately evasive.

"Dinner, Emily?"

She studied him. Jacob Stone trying to be gently persuasive was an interesting sight. It was obviously very difficult for him. It was also strangely endearing in a way Emily could not quite explain. She had harbored a secret passion for him for so long, she reflected in quiet wonder. How could she possibly turn down an invitation from him?

"All right," she agreed rashly. "Maybe you do owe me a meal." She stuffed several more bunches of flowers into the cooler and closed the sliding glass door. "What time do you want to pick me up?"

"Seven?" His gray eyes, normally so cold and bleak, were lit with the fires of a latent anticipation now.

She smiled wryly. "You're in luck. As it happens, I'm free at seven tonight."

There was definite satisfaction in Jacob's expression as he nodded his head. "Thanks, Emily."

"For what?"

"For giving me a chance." He turned and started to walk out of the shop. A fern caught his eye and he paused to examine it. His big hand lifted to touch one delicate frond. He seemed momentarily fascinated by the lacy greenery. Then he dropped his hand and went on out of the shop without a backward glance.

Emily stared after him, aware that she had been holding her breath as she watched him touch the frond with careful fingers. For a moment there she had witnessed a hint of the capacity for tenderness that lay buried far beneath the granite-hard exterior of the man. She had sensed that gentle streak in him the first time she had met him. It had always been a mystery to her that no one else ever seemed aware of it, including Jacob himself.

Then she went on to question her own rashness in accepting his dinner invitation.

There was a fine line between being bold and assertive and being reckless. Emily had a hunch she had just crossed the boundary.

THE EVENING did not start out auspiciously, and it was all Jacob Stone's fault.

Emily had taken pains with her dress selection, finally opting for a black-and-white two-piece outfit that emphasized the contrast of her black hair and fair skin. The long-sleeved top had a dropped waistline that rode her hips in a sophisticated, sensual manner. The skirt was a flared froth of silk that moved easily around her legs. Silver earrings gleamed from under the fall of her jet-black hair. The black frames of her glasses gave her amber eyes a mysterious, watchful quality.

Jacob arrived at her door wearing a dark jacket, a conservative white shirt and dark trousers. His hair had been brushed severely into place and his shoes had been laboriously shined. He had on a tie that was as conservative as the rest of his attire. It appeared to have been tied in a rather painful knot. Jacob Stone might be dangerously resourceful when it came to resolving an untenable business situation, but when it came to clothes, he obviously had decided long ago to take no chances.

But the conservatism of his clothing was only the second impression Emily received when she opened the door. The first, almost overwhelming, factor that hit her with the force of a blow was the sensual hunger in his gaze. His cloud-colored eyes gleamed with gray fire for an instant before he managed to bank the flames. Emily was jolted by it—almost frightened. For a few seconds she actually considered slamming the door and locking it again.

As if he read her thoughts, Jacob casually put a foot over the threshold. "You look very lovely tonight, Emily." He smiled crookedly. "I wanted to bring flowers, but I didn't know what kind would impress a lady whose business was flowers."

Emily eyed him uncertainly and then realized that his eyes appeared normal again. Perhaps she had just imagined that flare of raw masculine hunger. She smiled in spite of herself. "So what did you bring instead of flowers?"

He blinked, clearly nonplussed, and looked involuntarily down at his empty hands. "Uh, nothing. Just myself. Sorry. I . . . Are you ready?"

She nodded, taking pity at his obvious discomfort. "I'm ready." Poor Jacob. She wondered how a man who was such a whiz at knocking heads together both literally and figuratively could be so awkward socially. Then again, maybe it made perfect sense. Head bashing and proper social manners probably did not go well together.

It was as they stepped into the elevator that Jacob asked the question that nearly put a halt to the whole evening.

"Have you told Morrell you won't be seeing him again?"

Emily's mood darkened instantly. "If you want us both to enjoy this evening, I suggest you do not discuss Damon Morrell."

Jacob's eyes narrowed as he punched the lobby button. He looked prepared to argue the point, but something—common sense, perhaps—stopped him. "You're not a fool, Emily. I know that. I'll assume you've done what needed to be done. If you don't want to talk about it, that's fine with me."

She smiled triumphantly back at him, pleased by the small victory. "Thank you. I assure you, I do not want to talk about Damon. Now, where are we going for dinner?"

"I got a recommendation from the front desk at my hotel." Jacob named the popular restaurant located in the Pike Place Market complex. "Is that all right?"

"Oh, yes. It sounds perfect. What are we going to talk about all evening now that we've agreed not to discuss Damon?"

Jacob shrugged and smiled. "Us?"

"I'm not sure I want to discuss us, either. I'd rather talk about you."

He folded his arms and leaned back against the elevator wall. He seemed very massive in the small, confined space. "What do you want to know about me?" he asked with a frown.

"I think," Emily said slowly, "that I would like to know what's been happening to you for the past couple of years."

"That makes us even," he remarked as the elevator doors slid open. "I'm very curious about what you've been doing for the past two years, also."

"Mostly I've been busy causing my family no end of concern about my future," Emily said lightly as they walked out through the lobby to a Mercedes parked at the curb. "They were totally traumatized when Grandmother left me her shares in RI. But they recovered slightly when it became clear I didn't really intend to interfere in the running of the firm. They don't like the situation but they've learned to live with it."

"Your grandmother was one hell of a lady," Jacob said reminiscently. "I liked her."

"She drove the others nuts every time she took an active interest in RI. She always wanted to be certain the company was operating ethically. She claimed Ravenscrofts were predators by nature and had to be kept under control. At any rate, after the family stopped trying to get me to surrender my interest in RI they went back to fretting about my career choice. They're all hoping the flower business will prove to be a temporary aberration on my part."

"Like the notion of going off to join an artists' colony when you were eighteen?"

Emily grimaced. "Mother told you about that, did she? Well, I'm sorry to disappoint her, but I'm afraid that this time I'm sticking with my decision. I suppose I should have known better than to think I was actually being invited down to Portland to discuss my plans for opening a new shop. I ought to have realized my family is not about to loan me any money for expanding my business. I really walked right into that trap Friday night, didn't I? Talk about being set up."

Jacob gave her an impatient glance as he helped her into the dark Mercedes. Then he went around the front and slid behind the wheel. He sat quietly for a moment, staring out into the street. Emily felt the tension in him, and she knew he had himself under tight control.

"It wasn't a trap or a setup, Emily. Your father asked you to come to Portland to discuss business. He considered your relationship with Morrell as a genuine threat to Ravenscroft and to you personally. He wanted the issue settled quickly and cleanly. Don't blame him or your brother, or your mother. They've always operated in a very straightforward style. You know that. They don't dither around and anguish over things. When they see a clear and present danger, they act."

"Without any regard for the feelings of others. Yes, I know."

"How long are you going to blame me for my part in what happened?" Jacob eased the car away from the curb and started toward First Avenue. As they drove down toward the water, the lights on Elliott Bay glittered in the darkness.

"I've decided there's no point blaming you," Emily said gently. "That's why I agreed to come out with you tonight. You only did what you had to do. I understand. My family can be very demanding."

He shot her an astonished glance. "Do you mean that? You're not going to hold any of it against me?"

"Don't worry. The days are gone when they used to kill the messenger who brought bad news. That's all you were. The messenger. I'm sorry my family felt compelled to drag you into this mess."

"Mind telling me why you're suddenly being so understanding and forgiving about my role in the matter? I'm not complaining, but I am a little baffled. Friday night when I left you I got the feeling you would like to have put me through the Ravenscroft corporate paper shredder."

"Let's just say that in the cold light of day, I put things back into perspective. I've had the weekend to think about things. I know how my family operates," she went on soothingly. "They don't hesitate to call in a few favors when it suits them."

"Emily, I'll say this one more time and that's all. What I did, I did for your sake. I know it was a rough way to get the news about Morrell, but I agreed with your family. We all wanted to make it quick and clean."

"Let's not talk about why you did what you did. I don't want to talk about that any more than I want to talk about Damon."

"If you're willing to put the matter behind us, then I guess I am, too. Where does that leave us, Emily?"

"On the way to dinner."

"Right." Jacob smiled and made an obvious effort to relax. "Tell me about the flower shop."

"Are you really interested?"

"I'm interested in everything about you, Emily."

So she told him about Emily's Garden. When he proved astonishingly interested, she gave him all the gory details, including how she had sold her car and taken out a loan from a bank to go into business for herself nearly two years ago. Her family had refused to help her finance the shop, so Emily had sought out her own financing. She had only recently been able to afford another vehicle.

"You can imagine what my folks said when they found out what I'd done. They've been opposed to my decision to make a career in the florist business right from the start. They've done everything they could to discourage me. Grandmother Ravenscroft was the only one who actually encouraged me."

"What made you think your family might be willing to finance the second shop?"

Emily sighed. "I was hoping that the fact that I've made a success out of the first shop would alleviate some of their concerns about my business abilities. I'm turning a profit and I've proved I can run a business. It was dumb, I know, but I thought I'd give them another chance. Looks like I was wasting my time, though. I'll have to go back to the bank for the loan I need."

"You never gave your father a chance to discuss the loan," Jacob reminded her. "You stormed out of the house before anyone ever got to that subject."

Emily allowed herself a short, humorless laugh. "Let's just say that after having let myself get tricked into that embarrassing confrontation in the study, I didn't see much point in sticking around. I seriously doubt that my family ever had any real intention of discussing my business plans. They just let me believe they were willing to talk about the loan as a ruse to get me down to Portland. I should have know better." Emily shook her head. "One of these days I'll learn. I've gotten a lot better at handling them during the past couple of years, but once in a while I still get caught in the same old traps."

"Is that how you see your family's concern for you? A trap?" Jacob asked disapprovingly.

"I realize that in their own way they do love me and they honestly want what they think is best for me. If I didn't believe that, I wouldn't put up with them at all. But they are basically a bunch of single-minded, arrogant, ruthless business people whose main goal in life is the perpetuation and glory of Ravenscroft International. Grandmother was right. They're natural business predators. On top of that, they all seem to think they were born with some divine right to run my life as well as the life of everyone else who gets within striking distance. You should know what I'm talking about. You've had the misfortune to work for them for several years."

"Emily, I think you're overstating the case," Jacob said forcefully as he parked the car on the street in front of the restaurant. "I'll grant you that Gifford and Drake can be single-minded when it comes to running RI and maybe they do tend to think they know what's best for you. But let's face it, your track record—with men, at least— hasn't been exactly reassuring. Is it any wonder they get involved in your love life when you insist on falling for men like Brad Carlton and Damon Morrell?"

Emily's smile thinned. She watched him warily as he switched off the car's engine. Then she relaxed slightly as she realized what was happening. "It's all right, Jacob," she said gently. "I understand how it is. You've been very loyal for a long time and old habits are hard to break. But there's no need to defend my family to me. I know exactly what they are and how they operate. I was a fool to think of approaching them for that loan in the first place. I should have known better. And I can understand how you got manipulated by them this time around."

Jacob stared at her. "How I got manipulated by them?" he repeated, sounding honestly baffled.

"It's all right." Emily patted his sleeve reassuringly as she started to open her door. "You don't have to explain it to me. We're both victims of my family, and we're both going to find a way to get completely out of their clutches one of these days. Maybe the trick is for us to stick together."

"Emily..."

She smiled kindly. "Do you know that I used to think of you as a sort of professional enforcer for Ravenscroft International? When my family sent you to buy off Brad Carlton, I told myself you were nothing more than a paid mercenary for RI. Friday night I was so angry that I told myself nothing had changed. But now I realize you were as trapped by your old loyalties as I was trapped in my role of dutiful daughter. But we've both taken steps to free ourselves from my family. We're on our way, Jacob. Maybe together we can accomplish what neither one of us can quite manage alone. Maybe we can finally get out from under their shadows."

"Emily! Dammit, wait a minute..."

Jacob surged out of the car as she stepped out onto the sidewalk. He was beginning to feel as if he were falling down the rabbit hole. Emily was not reacting the way he had anticipated.

He had expected anything from more tears and accusations to a stony silence. He had been prepared to handle either extreme, but what he was getting had not been on his list of possibilities.

Jacob could have sworn Emily was feeling sorry for him. She seemed to be offering sympathy—a sort of comrades-in-arms affection.

It occurred to him that though sympathy was not what he wanted from her it might make a good starting point for building a more passionate relationship. He took her arm as he caught up with her.

"Emily," he said urgently as he steered her into the restaurant, "maybe it would be best if we didn't discuss your family for a while. Let's just concentrate on getting to know each other again, all right?"

She smiled brilliantly up at him with her eyes and Jacob thought he would drown in amber. His whole body was suddenly tight and hot and vibrating with need. For a tantalizing instant he allowed himself to fantasize about carrying her out of the restaurant, driving her back to her apartment and making love to her in the middle of her white-carpeted living room. He could just picture her lying there with flowers scattered around her. He could feel himself inside her, taking her, having her, loving her.

"All right," Emily said willingly enough.

Jacob groaned, knowing she was agreeing to his earlier question about getting to know each other, not to his silent, searing fantasy. Patience, he told himself. He had to have patience. Things were going very well—better than he'd had any right to expect. He could use her budding sense of sympathy to lead her into a warmer relationship.

"Thank you, Emily." Jacob spoke with genuine gratitude. He kept his hold on her softly rounded arm as the host showed them to a table.

Three hours later, as Jacob stood in the hall outside her apartment and wished Emily good-night, he mentally cursed his decision to practice patience. Intellectually he knew it was the right one. He had to give Emily time to adjust to the idea of thinking of him as a lover.

They had made great progress tonight, he decided as he rode the elevator back down to the lobby. Emily had actually begun to treat him as a friend.

She had chatted easily about her work and his, as well
as a variety of other subjects. She seemed quite willing
to get to know him as a man who had other aspects to
his personality besides the ability to be a paid "enforcer"
for Ravenscroft International. Jacob winced at the description.

But it was going to be tough to be patient. The dull,
restless aching sensation in his lower body made him
vividly aware of just how tough. He did not want to give
himself cheerful little lectures on how much progress he
was making with Emily. What he really wanted to do was
spend the night in Emily's bed. Five years was a long time
to wait for a woman.

She apparently thought of him as a muscle-brained hit
man, but he thought of her as an intriguing, exotic flower
that had blossomed from the sweet little bud he had first
met five years ago.

Jacob was tormenting himself with more fantasies and
a lot of hard-edged plans when he walked out of the
empty lobby and onto the sidewalk. Preoccupied with
his thoughts, he climbed into his car and automatically
turned the key in the ignition.

He would not have noticed the dark car that had been
parked behind his own vehicle if it had not pulled away
from the curb at the same time he did. But bright headlights flared briefly in his rearview mirror for an instant,
and Jacob instinctively noted them.

Three blocks later the dark car was still behind him. It
had fallen behind two other vehicles but it was still there.

Jacob looked for it again when he eased into the hotel
parking garage. This time when he glanced into the mirror, there was no sign of the other car.

A coincidence, he told himself calmly. But he made a mental note and filed it away in the corner of his brain he reserved for just such coincidences.

Good professional "enforcers" needed such internal filing systems, he thought wryly. Emily would nod understandingly if she knew about his personal records storage and retrieval mechanism.

It bothered Jacob that there might have been an element of truth in her mental image of him. But he remembered the gentle light of empathy in her eyes tonight and decided that he would work with that. One of these days she would be his.

4

SOMEWHAT TO HER SURPRISE, Emily enjoyed the next few days. She began anticipating Jacob's arrival at the shop at lunch and again after work. He seemed contented to occupy himself during the hours when she was busy and eager to spend every available minute with her when she was not. He even offered to give her and Diane a hand around the shop and showed a surprising interest in the flowers being arranged and sold.

On at least two occasions during a customer rush, Jacob made cross-town deliveries using Emily's little station wagon. The first time he returned to the shop with a huge grin on his face. It was so strange to see him with such an expression that Emily stared at him in utter confusion.

"What happened?" she demanded.

He pulled two dollar bills out of his pocket and proudly displayed them on the counter. "I got a tip. The lady was so thrilled that someone had sent her flowers that she tipped the guy who delivered them. By the time I realized what was happening, she'd already closed the door."

Emily echoed his grin. "You see, not everyone wants to kill the messenger. The trick is to bring flowers instead of depressing news."

Jacob looked down at her. "I'll remember that." It was a promise.

Before Emily could think of a response, Jacob had walked into the small room at the back of the shop where boxes of fresh-cut flowers had recently been stacked by the wholesaler. He was familiar with the routine now, and Emily heard him go to work unpacking the flowers. She smiled to herself, thinking of how carefully he handled the delicate product she sold. There was no danger to the blooms when they were in Jacob's strong hands.

She had a fleeting image of him holding a baby as tenderly as he held a bunch of orchids and quickly put the picture out of her mind. The last thing she wanted to do at this stage was to look into the future.

Diane found Jacob and his steady pursuit of Emily vastly amusing.

"The man's falling all over himself trying to please you," she told Emily one morning before Jacob arrived. "It's so sweet. And such an excellent position in which to have a man. I love to see them panting like that. When are you going to start being nice to him?"

Emily blinked in astonishment. She paused in the middle of attaching a purple-and-white tulip to an invisible wire that would hold it in position in the arrangement she was creating. "What on earth are you talking about? I am nice to him."

"I mean, when are you going to put him out of his misery and go to bed with him?" Diane explained with mocking patience. "For that matter, when are you going to let him move in with you? The man's living in a hotel, for crying out loud. Have you any idea what that costs?"

Emily flushed and rammed the wired tulip into place. "My relationship with Jacob is absolutely none of your business."

"You're thinking about getting him out of that hotel, though, aren't you?" Diane asked slyly. "I can see the sparkle in your eyes every time he walks into the shop. I must admit, I never saw that particular glitter when Damon Morrell came around. Or any other man during the past two years, for that matter. Jacob Stone is different, isn't he?"

"Jacob and I are friends," Emily said loftily as she wired another flower.

"Sure. And one of these days you're going to be lovers. Watch out, Emily. The next thing you know, you'll be thinking of marriage."

"Not a chance." Something happened to the tulip in Emily's hands. It crumpled in spite of the thin wire that was meant to hold it straight. She must have handled it too roughly, she realized.

Diane eyed her friend curiously. "How can you be so sure there's no future with him?"

"I didn't say there was no future, I just said there was no chance of marriage." Emily concentrated on wiring another tulip to take the place of the one that had just collapsed. This time she would be more careful.

"Why?" Diane asked baldly.

"For one thing, Jacob once told me he would never marry again."

"Men change their minds."

Emily shook her head. "Not Jacob. And even if he did, marriage would be out of the question for us. I don't even want to think about what my family might do if they thought I was going to marry Jacob Stone."

Diane looked at her seriously. "You think they would try to put a stop to it?"

"Of course. They would never approve of him in a million years."

"They employed him. From what you've told me they trusted him with Ravenscroft secrets. Your family seems to like him."

"That's got nothing to do with it," Emily said wryly. "The fact that he was once a trusted employee would not make him a good candidate for my husband in their eyes. My family has very definite ideas about the kind of man I should marry, and if I look as if I'm going to choose the wrong one, they'll do something about it."

"Like what?"

Emily shuddered and tried to speak lightly. "Oh, it depends. Buy him off or warn him off or find a way to prove he's only after my interest in RI. Whatever works. My family is very practical and straightforward in such matters." She knew some of her bitterness had leaked into her words.

"You think they could buy off Jacob? Or warn him off? Or even prove he's after your shares and your seat on the board? I'm not so sure about that, Emily. Your Mr. Stone looks very solid to me. It would take a lot to deflect him from any course of action he chooses to take. It's hard to deflect a chunk of rock."

"I'm not sure what they would try with Jacob, but believe me, they'd find something. I know my family."

"What will they do if they find out you're just having an affair with him?" Diane pressed.

"I'm not having an affair with him." *Not yet, at any rate,* she added silently, aware of the thrill of anticipation that shot through her at the thought.

"But if you do get involved in that way?" Diane persisted.

Emily hesitated, gnawing on her lower lip. "The best thing for all concerned would be for them not to find out," she finally decided softly, thinking it through. "If

I were to have an affair with Jacob, I would keep it very, very quiet. When dealing with my family, discretion is definitely the better part of valor." And the last thing she would want to do would be to risk losing Jacob.

Diane was unwilling to give up her point. "But what if your family eventually found out about him?"

Emily groaned. "They'd hit the roof."

"Really?"

"You can bet they wouldn't like the idea one bit. I think they'd be almost as upset about that as they would be about my marrying him. Almost, but not quite. After all, an affair isn't a permanent arrangement, in their view. It's marriage they worry about. Marriage puts my RI shares in jeopardy. Marriage means in-laws and another family getting involved in RI business. Marriage means there might be kids from an unapproved sire who would stand to inherit my interests in RI. Mustn't have that. The family name and business must be protected."

"But a quiet little affair . . . ?"

Emily drummed her fingers on the counter, thinking about that. "There's a chance, just a chance, mind you, that I could manage an affair with Jacob without bringing down the wrath of the Ravenscrofts on both our heads. If I'm discreet and very, very careful."

"You've got that funny look in your eyes again," Diane observed. "You know what I think?"

"What?"

"I think you're falling in love with Jacob Stone."

Emily suddenly felt very vulnerable. "I think I'd better get this arrangement done or forget about the Strandburg account altogether."

By applying a stupendous amount of willpower, Emily managed not to think about having an affair with Jacob for the rest of the afternoon. She steadfastly put the whole notion out of her mind while she worked, determined not to let it distract her.

But later that evening as she dressed for dinner, the sense of anticipation within her blossomed forth again. Emily looked at herself in the mirror as she put on a pair of silver-and-turquoise earrings and thought about her uncertain future with Jacob.

She was in love with the man. She had loved him in various ways for five years. Now that he was back in her life, that love was stronger than ever. Sooner or later, if Jacob hung around, she was going to wind up in an affair with him.

If that happened, she would be skating on very thin ice and she knew it. Her family would not like the idea at all.

She had been right when she had told Diane that having a love affair with Jacob Stone would require enormous caution and discretion. In fact, the only safe way to manage it would be to keep the affair a complete secret.

Emily shuddered, thinking of the logistics of trying to keep an affair with Jacob a secret from her family. Still, other people had secret affairs. History was full of such liaisons. It could be done. At least for a while.

The doorbell rang just as Emily was wondering dismally how long she could keep an affair hidden from her ever-vigilant family. She would need Jacob's full cooperation, and he was not the most subtle of men.

She walked to the door, expecting Jacob to be in the hall. He frequently showed up early for a date. It was flattering, but it was also a bit unsettling. Emily got the feeling Jacob enjoyed prowling around her apartment while waiting for her to finish dressing.

Certain that it was Jacob ringing her doorbell, Emily opened the door without bothering to double-check the identity of her visitor. It was a shock to see who stood in the hall.

"Damon!"

"Hello, Emily." Damon Morrell smiled fleetingly as he stood looking down at her. The expression did not reach his blue-green eyes. His tawny brown hair was attractively ruffled, he was dressed in an expensive European cut jacket and slacks. Unlike Jacob, he wore a silk tie with aplomb. "May I come in?" he asked politely.

"I'm about to go out," Emily explained, feeling extremely wary. She had been hoping to avoid a face-to-face confrontation with Damon. He was big, almost as tall as Jacob, although he did not give the impression of solidity that Jacob did. Damon had a leaner, wirier build. It was that build that enabled him to wear Italian fashions with consummate ease.

"I want to talk to you."

"Some other time," she suggested a little too brightly.

"Now, Emily. I want to talk to you now. Tonight." Damon pushed open the door and stepped through into the hall.

Emily's sense of uneasiness took a quantum jump. She instinctively backed off a couple of steps and then tried to hold her ground. Her chin came up angrily and her eyes narrowed. "What is this all about, Damon?"

"That's what I'm trying to find out," he replied, closing the door behind him. "You've been avoiding me for nearly a week. I'd like to know why."

"I don't owe you any explanations." Emily forced herself to speak calmly and quietly.

"You're seeing someone else."

"Am I?" Turn the question around. That was one of the tactics she had been taught in her assertiveness training course.

He ignored that and strode past her into the living room. Emily watched helplessly, wondering how to go about throwing him out.

"I would like you to leave, Damon." Emily stood stiffly in the hall and told herself she had to keep calm and in control of the situation.

"Not until I get some answers." Damon crossed through the white-on-white living room and came to a halt near the window. He thrust his hands into his pockets and stood staring out at the street below. "You changed after you came back from Portland. You haven't accepted any of my invitations since your return. Something happened down there, didn't it? What was it, Emily?"

"I'd rather not discuss our past relationship, such as it was," Emily said, calling on her training again. It would be better not to get into an argument with him. Better to keep things cool and businesslike.

"What did you discover about me down in Portland that changed your whole attitude?" Damon prodded quietly.

"I've told you, I don't want to discuss it. Please leave, Damon."

"I'm not leaving here until I know what went wrong between us." He kept his gaze focused on the lighted street outside the window.

Emily sighed. The part of her that had always dreaded confrontations was cringing now. But maybe the man did deserve an explanation. "I think you must know what went wrong."

"Tell me."

"I found out about a woman named Marcia, for one thing," Emily said bluntly. "I also found out that you had plans to use me to try to destroy Ravenscroft International. There—does that answer your questions?"

Damon swung around to confront her. There was an expression in his eyes that Emily had never seen before. It was hard and angry. But when he spoke, his voice was remote. "I wondered if that might be it."

Emily winced. "You're not even going to bother to deny it?"

Damon shrugged. "There is a woman named Marcia, although she's not important."

"I'll bet she'd be interested in learning that," Emily said scathingly.

"Marcia is no innocent. She knows how the game is played."

"Apparently I was not so smart," Emily retorted rashly, forgetting all her assertiveness training as her own anger surged to the fore. "I actually believed you were interested in me because you liked me, not because you wanted to get your hands on my RI shares. I didn't even realize you knew who I was. It was very depressing finding out you planned to use me, Damon. I'm sure you can understand why I lost interest in developing our relationship."

Damon began to pace back and forth in front of the windows. "Your family did some investigating, I suppose, after they discovered you were dating me?"

"Yes."

"And you believed everything they told you?"

Emily drew a deep breath and clasped her hands behind her back. "My family is frequently overbearing, ruthless and domineering, but they have never, ever lied to me. In fact, they tend to be brutally honest most of the time. Yes, I believed the evidence I was given. I didn't want to believe it, but I had no real choice. Just out of curiosity, would you mind telling me why you're so eager to hurt RI?"

"Your brutally honest family didn't tell you?" Damon asked dryly.

Emily shook her head. "No. They said it had to do with business. Something about a bidding war between your firm and RI."

Damon's mouth curved cruelly. "Didn't that make you curious?"

"My family doesn't confide business secrets to me unless it's absolutely necessary," Emily said grimly. "They think I'm a little too naïve and innocent to handle the sordid details of the big-time business world."

"They're right," Damon said with surprising alacrity. "You're a lamb among wolves, my sweet. The rest of the Ravenscrofts must think they were given a changeling when you were born. An innocent little elf slipped into the crib in exchange for a true-blooded, fire-breathing Ravenscroft. You certainly don't belong in that family."

"But you found me very useful, nevertheless, didn't you, Damon?"

He stopped pacing and looked at her. "I also found you very sweet and very desirable."

Emily flinched. "If you think you can soothe my wounded pride by telling me you actually wanted me, not just my shares, forget it. I'm not that dumb or that naïve."

He took a step toward her. "It's true, Emily. I'll admit I got involved with you originally because I saw you as a means of gaining access to power within RI. But the more I got to know you, the more I wanted you. I was trying to court you, Emily. I was taking it slow and easy because I didn't want to scare you off. I thought we had time. I should have known your family would be keeping close tabs on you and anyone you started dating seriously."

Emily ignored that. "Are you going to tell me why you wanted a chunk of RI so badly that you were willing to try to seduce and marry me to get it?"

"You make it sound very cold-blooded."

"Wasn't it?"

Damon smiled faintly. "It might have started out that way, but it wasn't going to end that way. I was going to enjoy making love to you, Emily."

"No," Emily said calmly, "you wouldn't have enjoyed it because it was never going to happen."

Damon arched his eyebrows, obviously mildly amused. "You don't think I could have gotten you into bed eventually?"

"I don't love you, Damon. I had fun with you. I liked your companionship and I considered you a friend. But I was not falling in love with you."

"You just needed a little more time," he said with great certainty. "If your family hadn't interfered, things would have worked out exactly the way I wanted them to work out."

"No." Emily was absolutely certain of that. She had never been in any danger of falling in love with Damon Morrell, although Damon and her family and Jacob all apparently thought she was. It made her realize how little these iron-willed, autocratic, predator types really knew her. They were so accustomed to thinking of her as weak and vulnerable and helpless, so accustomed to thinking of her as *prey*, that they had never realized she had her own strengths and abilities and a measure of common sense.

"Emily, listen to me," Damon said persuasively. "You don't owe your family anything. All they care about is controlling your shares in RI."

"You should know. That's all you care about, too."

"You're wrong," Damon told her. "I also care about you. I won't deny I'd like to see RI on the rocks, but I—"

Emily held up a palm to stop him. "Please, Damon. Just leave."

"Not yet." He began walking toward her, his eyes suddenly intent. "I want to make sure you understand something first."

"What?" Emily jerked back in alarm as he reached for her. She didn't move quickly enough. Damon's hands closed around her and he pulled her roughly against him.

"Let me go, dammit," she ordered, becoming annoyed.

"I'm not going to let you kick me out of your life at this stage of the game," Damon vowed. "I've invested a lot of time and effort in you and I want the payoff. Damned if I'm going to let you get away with ruining everything. I should have moved more quickly with you. I can see that now. I gave you too much time and too much room. I should have taken you right at the start. If I had, you would have been right where I wanted you by now."

Things were getting out of hand, Emily decided. She planted both her palms against his shoulders and shoved with all her strength as Damon tried to crush her mouth beneath his own. She turned her head aside and swore in exasperation and anger.

"I said, *let me go*," Emily snapped. If he refused, she would have to do something more forceful, she realized. Matters weren't out of control yet, but they were definitely escalating. Damon pinned her body against his own. She aimed a swift, warning kick and managed to connect with his shin. He muttered something under his breath, but he did not release her.

At that moment the door slammed against the wall and Jacob exploded into the hall in a silent rush. Emily didn't even realize he was in the room until she suddenly found herself free. She was released so abruptly that she spun back against the wall. She opened her eyes in time to see Damon hit the floor with a resounding thud.

"Take your hands off her, Morrell." The command was dangerously soft. Jacob moved to stand over his victim, feet braced, his face set in a savage battle mask. His gray eyes were as cold and hard as granite. In that moment it was very easy to see that Stone was more than just a name to be applied to him. It was also an excellent description of the man himself. "Don't ever touch her again. If you do, I'll take you apart. Slowly. Now get out of here."

Damon rolled to his feet and got up cautiously, his eyes never leaving Jacob's face. There was wariness in him as he weighed and judged his adversary, but there was also a seething anger.

"I don't let anyone get in my way," Damon said. "Not for long. Not when I want something very badly. Remember that, Stone."

"If you know who I am, then you probably also know that I don't let people get in my way, either. Let's call it a draw this time around, Morrell. Cut your losses. You've got other fish to fry. Emily and her shares in RI are not on the menu."

Damon's gaze flicked briefly to Emily's taut features, then he concentrated on the real source of danger in the room. "I get the picture now. You're doing a little fishing for yourself. You're the one who should be cutting his losses, Stone. The Ravenscrofts aren't going to let you within a mile of Emily or her shares. You're playing out of your league."

"Get out of here, Morrell."

Damon's mouth curved derisively as he turned toward the door without another word. But as he stepped out into the hall, he spared Emily one last glance.

"A lamb among wolves," he muttered.

And then he was gone.

Emily, who had been frozen in place against the wall as she watched the small scene of violence played out, felt like collapsing. She closed her eyes and drew a deep, steadying breath. She was aware that her pulse was beating very rapidly and her nerves felt stretched with tension. She heard Jacob close the door.

"What the hell was he doing here, Emily?"

Emily opened her eyes to find her rescuer looking every bit as dangerous as the man who had just left. It took an act of willpower to summon her defenses as she realized she was now under a different kind of attack. It wasn't fair.

"What do you think he was doing here?" She straightened away from the wall, absently massaging her wrist. Damon had wrenched it at some point during the proceedings. "He came to see me."

"Why?" Jacob braced one hand against the wall beside her and planted his other fist on his hip as he scowled down at her.

Emily frowned resentfully. "He wanted to know why I had been finding excuses not to see him lately."

"Finding excuses?" Jacob's eyes narrowed dangerously. "You've been inventing excuses not to see him? You didn't tell him flat out that you never wanted to see him again?"

"I was trying to handle things gracefully," Emily tried to explain, feeling pressured now. "I thought he'd get the point without my having to humiliate both him and myself with a major confrontation scene."

"Emily, you are a little idiot!" Jacob grated. "Your family is right—you can't take care of yourself. Whatever made you think you could deal with someone like Morrell by inventing a series of weak excuses not to continue seeing him? You have to hit a man like that straight between the eyes and show him that you mean what you say."

"You and my family do things one way and I do them another."

"Is that right? Well, just look where your way got you. If you'd been blunt and forceful with Morrell the minute you came back from Portland, he would have realized the game was over then and there. Instead, you played coy and dragged things out. No wonder he came prowling around wondering what had gone wrong with his big plan."

"I did not play coy!" Emily blazed. "I resent that. I told you, I was trying to handle things without a major knock-down drag-out scene. What's more, I could have handled Damon just fine if you hadn't come charging through the door like a maddened rhino. I can take care of myself these days."

"Sure you can. That's why you were getting yourself pawed when I arrived," Jacob shot back. "You don't know the first thing about handling someone like Morrell." He slapped the wall with his open palm in a gesture of frustrated fury. "I knew I should have dealt with him and not left it up to you. I was a fool to let you do it on your own. You need a keeper, Emily."

"Just because I have my own way of dealing with people and just because that way doesn't happen to be your way or the traditional Ravenscroft way doesn't mean I need a keeper, dammit!" She was infuriated. "Furthermore, after what I have just been through, I resent having you yell at me."

"Why in hell did you open the door to him?" Jacob demanded between set teeth.

"When the doorbell rang, I thought it was you."

"You should have checked."

"Even if I had checked, I would still have opened the door," Emily said recklessly. "I had no reason to think Damon would act the way he did. He's always been very much a gentleman."

"Well, now you know better, don't you?" Jacob came away from the wall and thrust one hand under the curve of Emily's thick black hair. He wrapped warm, strong fingers around the nape of her neck. "Men don't always behave like gentlemen when it comes to business and women. And here's another lesson for you to learn. A man who finds himself having to pull another man off his woman doesn't feel at all like a gentleman."

Emily's whole body was vibrating to the sensual tension that was suddenly gripping her. The source of that tension was Jacob. It was as if the frustrated male anger that had been pulsing through him was rapidly converting itself into another kind of emotion. And she was responding to it on a primitive, utterly feminine level.

"Jacob?" Her voice was suddenly soft and breathless as the resentment and anger went out of her. A dizzying sensation of longing swept through her as she studied the gray flames in his eyes. Without thinking, Emily raised her fingers to touch the hard planes of his face.

Jacob looked down into her face and saw the first flickering promise of her response. He could also see the uncertainty and confusion underlying the hint of passionate excitement, but he knew suddenly and beyond any doubt that he could overcome her doubts and misgivings.

Because deep down, she wanted him.

The knowledge that Emily truly desired him was the last straw for Jacob. He had intended to wait awhile before he coaxed her into bed. He had wanted to give her all the time she needed. But having to rescue her from Morrell had set up an emotional chain reaction that was sweeping aside his earlier, more cautious approach. She wanted him and he wanted her with an urgency that knew no bounds. He had waited long enough. Tonight he would claim her.

Jacob groaned and his hand tightened behind Emily's head. The skin of her nape was like silk beneath his fingers—warm, soft, exquisite silk. He could feel the small shiver of pleasure and need that went through her, heard the tiny cry that parted her lips and his own desire surged through his veins like fiery lava. As he was unable to resist any longer, his mouth came down on Emily's with abrupt, hungry insistence.

Passion flared into a roaring blaze, ignited by the smoldering flames of the other, equally elemental, emotions that had been driving him since he had come through the door and found Damon Morrell trying to assault Emily.

"Emily, honey, Emily, I want you so much. So sweet. So beautifully sweet. You're so soft and delicate. I'll take care of you. I'll be so gentle with you. I swear it." The words tumbled out of him as he explored her mouth. Jacob was only half aware of what he was saying. He only knew he wanted to reassure her and remove any lingering doubts she might have about giving herself to him.

Emily smiled up at him, a soft, shimmering smile that was radiant with her passion. "I trust you, Jacob. And I want you very much." Her fingertips trembled in his hair.

Jacob thought he would sink beneath the sensuous waves of that smile. Instead he tightened his hold on Emily and deepened the kiss into one of throbbing intimacy. He could taste her now as she willingly opened her mouth for him and he was intoxicated by the essence of her. His hands shook slightly as he removed her glasses and put them down on a nearby table. Then he began to undress her.

Emily did not try to resist him. She seemed shyly eager to be rid of her clothing. She was already fumbling with the buttons of his shirt. He carefully lifted the top of her black-and-white outfit over her head. When he saw the dainty scraps of silk that barely shielded her breasts he thought he would lose control then and there, and the realization shook him. The last time he had come this close to the edge with a woman had been the first time he had kissed Emily two years ago. That night he had fought an internal battle for control and he had won. It had cost him dearly, but he had won.

Tonight he did not have to wage war with himself. Tonight Emily would be his.

"You're going to drive me out of my mind," Jacob whispered as he struggled briefly with the catch of her tiny bra. He leaned his forehead against hers and watched as the silk fell away to reveal her breasts. She was a small woman, but beautifully shaped, he thought, half dazed. Her breasts were round and full and tipped with rosy nipples that were already budding into full flower. "You've been driving me out of my mind for the past two years. Did you know that?"

"Ah, Jacob, Jacob, I didn't know it would be like this. I've wanted you for so long." Emily managed to push his shirt off his shoulders, and then she leaned her head against his chest, savoring his heat.

Jacob twisted his fingers in her hair and lifted the thick, dark mass away from the back of her neck. He bent his head and kissed her nape. "Two years ago everything was wrong for us," he muttered. "But this time around, it's going to be different. This time around it's going to be right." He touched one of her nipples with his thumb, and a waterfall of satisfaction and excitement went through him as the tip of her breast grew taut. "It's going to be perfect."

He picked her up and went down on one knee and then he settled her gently on the thick white carpet.

A moment later Jacob's own clothes were lying in a heap on the floor. He lowered himself beside Emily and drew a questing fingertip down between her breasts to the gentle curve of her stomach. When he encountered the obstruction of her panty hose, he slid his hand under the nylon and swept the garment away.

She was totally nude at last, and Jacob felt almost light-headed as he drank in the sight of her. He stroked her, reveling in the feel of her soft skin and the way she arched beneath his hand.

"Jacob."

She said his name as if she were begging him for something. Jacob kissed her heavily, trying to tell her without words that he wanted to give her everything. He felt her palms glide over his bare back, shaping the contours of his shoulders and then sliding down the long muscles to his buttocks. The gentle exploration made him almost wild with desire.

"I wanted to make this first time between us last, but you've already got me to the edge, sweetheart," he told her hoarsely. "Put your arms around me and tell me again how much you want me."

"I want you, Jacob."

"Emily. *Emily.*" He slid his hand down into the warmth between her legs. The liquid fire in her was dazzling. Jacob parted her thighs, desperate to bury himself within her and let her consume him even as he claimed her. She trembled slightly as he began to fit the rigid shaft of his manhood to her softness. She was so small and delicate. Jacob swore under his breath, furious with his own leaping need. "I'm going too fast," he gasped, his fingers digging into her shoulders as he tried to check himself.

"No, it's all right. It's all right, Jacob. I need you. I need you now." Emily pulled him closer, showing him without words that she was ready for him.

Jacob caught his breath, tightened his grip on her and eased himself heavily into Emily's soft, clinging warmth. She shivered as she folded herself around him.

Jacob's last coherent thought before he lost himself in the rhythms of passion was that claiming Emily was like plunging himself into a pool of clinging, sun-drenched flowers.

5

EMILY STOOD in the bedroom doorway, a steaming cup of coffee in her hands, and stared in wonder at the big man sprawled across her bed. Jacob lay on his back, the white sheet and blanket in a tangle at his waist.

He appeared remarkably sexy, lying there against the pristine white pillows. Hard, powerful and dangerous. A half-tamed predator who had wandered into this pretty, feminine bedroom and claimed it and its owner for his own. His dark hair was tousled, and his broad shoulders looked tanned and strong against the snowy bedclothes.

Emily was half convinced she was still dreaming.

The night had been a time of magic and discovery for Emily. She was in love. Completely. Totally. Everything she had felt for Jacob in the past paled in comparison to the shining passion and love she felt now that she had finally lain in his arms.

She took a couple of hesitant steps into the room, her robe brushing the white carpet. She had run a brush quickly through her hair before going out into the kitchen to make coffee, but she knew it was still in some disarray.

Emily came to a halt at the foot of the white lacquer bed and studied her lover more intently. The gray morning light of a Seattle dawn was flowing in through the windows. Emily always slept with the blinds open. She liked light, even at night. Last night Jacob had made no objection. He seemed more than content to make love to her time and again in the reflected glow from the city outside the windows.

A small, thrilling shiver, an echo of last night's passionate excitement, rippled through Emily as she stood looking down at Jacob. She had never known what real passion was until last night. She had never known how hot love could burn until last night. If Jacob had taken her to bed two years ago before leaving her, she would have been far more devastated than she had been at the time.

Then again, she told herself, if he had made love to her that night two years ago, perhaps he would not have been able to leave her. Neither of them would ever know. It no longer mattered. What was past was past.

The sensual lessons of the night drifted once more through Emily's head. She had never before understood what it was to give herself completely to a man and have him respond with the same uninhibited generosity. In Jacob's arms Emily had learned what it was to feel both safe and free.

When Jacob had claimed her last night, Emily had been stunned at the wildness that had swept through her. She had not even suspected such a bold, reckless side to her own nature. She had gloried in Jacob's strength and in her own newfound feminine power. Jacob's eyes had gleamed with passionate satisfaction and delight when he succeeded in bringing Emily to the shattering climax of their union.

It came to Emily then that this relationship with Jacob was the most important thing in her life. And following on the heels of that thought came another very primitive realization.

She would do anything in the world to protect this man and the love that had burst into full flower within her last night.

Emily was still contemplating the power of her protective instincts and wondering how such a fierce, wild streak could have lain dormant within her all these years when Jacob stirred and opened his eyes.

"The perfect woman," he said with a lazy, wicked grin as he surveyed the cup in her hand. "All my life I've wanted to have my coffee served to me in bed."

Emily smiled a little shyly. "I had no idea your fantasy life was so exciting."

"Don't make fun of my fantasies. I've lived on them for a long time." Jacob sat up against the pillows, yawning hugely. He held out his hand, and Emily walked to the side of the bed and put the cup and saucer in his strong fingers. He took it from her and then looked up at her expectantly. When she just stood there looking back at him, he scowled with mock impatience. "You're supposed to accompany the coffee with a kiss."

"Oh. How would you know if you've never had coffee served to you in bed before?"

"Emily, my sweet, some things a man just knows by instinct."

"I see." Emily bent her head and brushed her mouth lightly against his. He tasted warm and wonderfully familiar. "How's that?" she demanded lightly as she lifted her head again.

"If I weren't holding this cup and saucer, I would show you where you have room for improvement."

"Is that right?" Emily retorted.

"Damned right." He took a long swallow of coffee. "Fortunately for you, I'm a patient teacher. And you're a fast learner. I figure we're going to get along fine."

"Who says I have to do all the learning in this relationship?" Emily paused as the word "relationship" slipped out. She was not at all sure Jacob would like the sound of that. She knew from what he had said two years ago that he would never marry again, but she was not certain how he felt about other types of commitments. It would break her heart if he wanted to stay fancy-free and relatively uninvolved while she was trying to conduct an affair with him.

Jacob was studying her face as if trying to read the thoughts that must have been flickering in her eyes. "Nobody says you have to do all the learning, sweetheart," he said gently. "I'm learning a few things myself."

"Such as?" she asked breathlessly.

He hesitated just a fraction of an instant, as if thinking better of whatever was on the tip of his tongue. He smiled instead. "Such as how good you feel in my arms." He set the cup and saucer on a white end table and reached out to pull Emily down across his lap. "So good." He nuzzled the sensitive area behind her ear.

Emily felt the hardness of his thighs and the unmistakable force of his arousal. Her arms twined around his neck and she snuggled closer. "I'm glad," she whispered. "Because you feel very good, too."

"Remember the first time I kissed you?" Jacob asked softly.

"You mean the first time I kissed you. How could I forget? I was shattered when you called a halt right in the middle of things and sent me home." Her voice was quietly accusing.

She remembered that night with aching clarity. She would always remember it. It had been the night Jacob had finally gotten word his divorce was final.

Leanna's growing discontent and restlessness had finally led her into infidelity. It was no secret when the marriage went on the rocks primarily because Leanna managed to blow the whole thing into a major scandal. She had taken a lover who was a local politician, and when the affair became public knowledge the newspapers had had a field day. Jacob had been the stoic victim.

Eventually Emily had learned from a casual remark her grandmother had made that the divorce was final. On the spur of the moment, she had bought a bottle of Scotch and driven over to Jacob's apartment.

She had found him alone, already a quarter way through his own bottle.

"I made a very embarrassing pass at you that night," Emily recalled with a sigh.

"I wasn't embarrassed," he said gently. "I wanted you so badly I nearly forgot all my good resolutions and took you to bed. You'll never know the full extent of the battle I fought with myself that night."

"I wish you hadn't fought so hard."

"Putting you in that cab that night was the hardest thing I'd ever done in my life," Jacob said, watching the emotions shift in her amber eyes. "I told myself I had no right to take you then."

"And now?" she prompted gently.

He smiled. "Now everything is different." He slipped the robe off her shoulders, revealing her nude body underneath. She was warm and flushed, and her breasts seemed to swell under his palm. His hand moved lower and slid around her hip to cup one curved buttock. Jacob squeezed gently, and Emily turned her head so that she could kiss his throat.

They sat like that for a few minutes, enjoying the feel of each other and the sweet ache of early-morning desire. But Jacob's aroused state finally demanded release.

"Come here, sweetheart," he murmured thickly as he pushed back the covers and settled her astride his thighs. "Finish what you started with that cup of coffee."

"Was it the coffee that did this?" she asked in pretended amazement as she felt his hardness probing her feminine secrets.

"Must have been." His fingers sank into her flanks as he eased her gently down.

Emily gasped as he began to enter her slowly and deliberately, as if he were determined to savor every millimeter of the experience. It was an exquisite form of sensual torture for her. Her nails made small half circles in his shoulders, and her eyes closed in anticipation as her body adjusted to the slow, thorough invasion.

"That's it, honey." Jacob's voice was husky with desire as he carefully completed the union, filling her completely. "That's perfect. Absolutely perfect. You feel so good."

He moved one hand from her hip and reached down to stroke her intimately. Emily cried out and clung to him as she had so often during the night. Her whole body contracted with passion.

"Jacob, oh, Jacob . . ."

"I know." He stroked her again. "Open your eyes, sweetheart. Look at me. I want to see the way you look at me when you take what I can give you."

She did and found herself gazing into the cloudy depths of his own gaze. She wanted to tell him she loved him but knew it was much too soon for such a declaration. She kissed him instead, wrapping her arms around him as he guided her into the slow, compelling pattern.

For long moments Emily hovered on the brink. The slow, taut sensation created by Jacob's movements was driving her wild. And then he touched her one last time with unerring skill and she gasped. Her whole body went briefly rigid, and then the waves of release washed over her.

She was aware of Jacob surging deeply into her as his own body tautened, and then she heard her name in a hoarse shout of satisfaction.

The morning was golden.

FOR THE NEXT FEW DAYS Emily hugged her newfound happiness to herself. Diane told her she positively glowed with it. Emily's world had never seemed so right. She and Jacob were together constantly. He had not yet moved out of the hotel and into her apartment, but she knew it was only a matter of time before the subject arose. She worried a little about that because if Jacob moved in with her it would be very difficult to keep her family in the dark about the relationship.

But she decided she would deal with that when the time came. For the moment she was contented to explore her own happiness.

The golden days came to an end within a week. Jacob had just finished making slow, lazy love to Emily one morning when the phone beside the bed rang shrilly.

Jacob sprawled back on the bed, carrying Emily with him. "Someone's timing is very bad," he muttered.

"Could have been worse," Emily pointed out cheerfully as she reached for the phone.

"True. But if it had been any worse I wouldn't have let you answer the phone." Jacob propped himself on one elbow, surveying her with naked possessiveness as she spoke into the receiver.

"Oh, hello, Mom." Emily drew a deep breath, very conscious of Jacob's nearness. All her earlier determination to protect him and their new relationship welled up within her. She sat up and pulled the covers around herself, trying to think clearly. It was difficult, given her pleasantly relaxed frame of mind.

"I just wanted to say hello," Catherine Ravenscroft said briskly. "And keep you posted on the plans for your father's birthday, of course. I've had some second thoughts about the caterer, but unfortunately it's too late to switch now. We'll just have to hope for the best. I had a serious talk with him yesterday and warned him I do not want any foul-ups such as the one I witnessed at that reception last week."

"I'm sure he won't foul up at Dad's birthday party," Emily said reassuringly. "He wouldn't dare after your 'serious talk.' Who did you get for the flowers?"

As she spoke, Jacob drew a lazy finger down Emily's arm. Then he leaned forward and dropped a warm kiss into the hollow of her shoulder. Emily wanted to nestle against him, but instead she pulled away and shook her head in silent protest. She had her hands full at the moment. Jacob, of all people, should know that it took one's complete attention to deal with a Ravenscroft, even when the topic was something as innocuous as a birthday party.

But he ignored her small warning and touched the tip of his tongue to her shoulder, tasting her as if she were a scoop if ice cream. Emily shivered in instinctive response and again tried to ease away from him. Jacob's eyes narrowed, but Emily didn't notice.

"Emily? What's the matter? Are you listening to me?"

"Yes, of course I'm listening, Mom. I was just . . . just juggling a cup of coffee. Who did you say is doing the flowers?"

"I told you. That local florist you recommended. Weren't you listening? I trust we can count on her."

"She'll do a great job. Sally won't let you down. I use her all the time when I send flowers to Portland for my clients." Emily stifled a gasp as Jacob deliberately slid his hand under the blanket and found her inner thigh. He began drawing slow circles.

"Emily?" Her mother's voice was crisp and demanding.

"Yes, Mom?"

"I asked you when you planned to arrive on the day of the party. I think it would be best if you got here in the early afternoon at the latest. You can supervise the flowers and give me a hand with the final details. There will be nearly two hundred people here, you know."

"Uh, I was thinking of driving down later in the afternoon," Emily hedged. She tightened her legs together to avoid Jacob's distracting touch. His fingers became more insistent.

"No, I think you had better arrange to be here around one,"·Catherine said decisively. As usual, having given the orders, she had no doubt but that they would be carried out. It was a typical Ravenscroft characteristic. "Are you bringing anyone with you to the party?"

Startled by the question, Emily paused. "Well, I hadn't thought much about it." She hadn't thought about it at all since she had been forced to dismiss Damon Morrell from her life. Jacob's hand continued to make erotic little circles on her thigh. He lowered his head and dropped a lingering kiss into the valley between her breasts. Emily sucked in her breath and glared at him. He ignored her.

But her mother did not. "Emily?" This time Catherine Ravenscroft's voice was quite sharp. "Is someone there with you?"

Emily looked at Jacob, who was ignoring her in favor of sinking his strong teeth quite gently into her upper leg. He seemed to like the taste of her.

"Emily, I asked you a question. Is someone there with you?"

Emily began to grow annoyed with her mother's tactless line of inquiry. Her family recognized very few boundaries to Emily's privacy. Maybe it was time they learned a lesson. "Why do you ask?"

"Because you sound distracted." Catherine's voice tightened with sudden tension. "Emily, is there a man with you?"

"You can hardly expect me to discuss that sort of thing on the phone, Mom."

But Catherine had already leaped to her own conclusions. "It's not Damon Morrell, is it?" she demanded ominously. "Surely you've got more sense than to continue your involvement with him after what we told you about him."

"Not to worry, Mom," Emily said brightly. "I don't plan to marry Damon. That was the chief concern, wasn't it? That I would marry him?"

"My God, Emily," her mother gasped. "You can't mean to say you're having an affair with him? After learning what kind of man he really is?"

"Don't worry, I won't say I'm having an affair with Damon," Emily agreed in a soothing voice that only alarmed her mother all the more. Emily smiled grimly to herself. "I'll keep my mouth shut if you do."

Jacob's head came up abruptly, all the teasing passion gone from his eyes as he realized exactly who and what was being discussed. His hand tightened on Emily's ankle as he straightened and scowled down at her.

"Emily! You can't possibly have him there with you!" Catherine was stunned at the implications. "Have you no common sense at all?"

"Mother, I've decided I don't like discussing my private life with my family. They tend to interfere. I'm sure you'll understand if I prefer not to continue this conversation. Say hello to Dad and Drake for me. I'll see you at Dad's birthday party." Emily hung up the phone in the middle of her mother's shocked silence. She smiled brilliantly at Jacob, pleased with herself for having protected him and for having struck a blow for her own independence at the same time.

But Jacob paid no attention to her high-voltage smile. He turned away from her, tossed back the covers and climbed out of bed. He stood glaring down at her, oblivious of his own nudity. His whole bearing was one of masculine aggression.

Emily's smile faded into wariness as she looked up at him. "Jacob? What's wrong?"

"What the hell was that all about?" he said through gritted teeth.

"You must have heard. That was my mother."

"Don't play dumb. I'm aware it was your mother. I meant what was all that drivel about making her think Morrell was in your bed this morning?"

"Oh, that." Emily smiled with some satisfaction. "I get so tired of my family interfering in my life, Jacob. Once in a while I can't resist the urge to retaliate. Mother was demanding to know if I had actually had the nerve to go to bed with Damon after the family had gone out of its way to forbid any connection with him. I decided I'd taken enough orders from Ravenscrofts."

"So you let her think you were sleeping with Morrell?" Jacob's face was tight with his anger. "What kind of a game do you think you're playing?"

Emily scrunched back against the headboard, pulling the covers up to her chin. She was offended. "I didn't do it just because I was feeling vengeful. I also did it to protect you."

"You did it to protect *me*?" Jacob was clearly astounded. "Have you gone nuts? What the hell did you think you were protecting me from?"

"My family!"

Jacob swore and leaned down to cage her between his hands. His eyes were swirling with gray storm clouds. "Now you listen to me and you listen good, lady. I can take care of myself. The day I need protection from your family or anyone else, I will tell you. Until then, you will let me take care of myself. Understood?"

"But, Jacob . . ."

"Forget it. I don't want any arguments. The subject is closed. Which brings us to the second topic on the agenda."

"What's that?" Emily asked uneasily.

"I'll be damned if I'll have your family or anyone else thinking you're sleeping with Damon Morrell. You're sleeping with me and you'd better make sure anyone who has an interest in the matter knows the truth. I don't want any more misconceptions, misinformation or mistakes on that subject."

Emily chewed on her lower lip, troubled. "I understand what you're saying and it's very sweet of you to want to be up-front about...about our relationship, but I'm not so sure it's a good idea to shout it from the rooftops. Especially to my family. You know as well as I do they can be difficult."

"Let me worry about your family. You concentrate on making sure no one leaps to any more false conclusions. Is that clear?"

Emily was hurt. "Of course it's clear. It could hardly be anything else but clear with the way you're yelling at me."

"I never yell." Each word was taken out of deep freeze.

That much was true, she thought with a sigh. Jacob was not exactly yelling. His voice was low, controlled and very dangerous. The truth was, he might have been less intimidating if he was yelling.

"I realize that your ego was probably punctured somewhat by my letting my mother think Damon was here instead of you, but I really think it would be for the best if we kept our...our, uh, relationship private," Emily said earnestly.

"Private? As in secret? You expect me to skulk around in the middle of the night, hoping no one notices me leaving your bed?" he asked incredulously. "You think you can keep an affair secret for long?"

"Well, an affair is a private matter, isn't it?" Emily countered quickly. "Why should everyone else have to know what's going on between us?"

"Because I damned well want everyone else to know!" Jacob straightened away from the bed and stalked toward the bathroom. He turned on the threshold and shot her one last, quelling look. "You belong to me now and I don't care who knows it. If you think I'm going to let you play games, you're out of your mind."

Emily was tired of feeling pressured. "If I want to play games, I will. I'm tired of my family and you giving me orders and telling me how to conduct my life."

"Is that right?" Jacob shot back coolly.

"Yes, that's right." She lifted her chin.

Jacob studied her for a long moment, as if wondering just how far she could be pushed this morning. Then his gaze softened. He smiled faintly. "Poor Emily. You always seem to be on the receiving end, don't you?"

"The receiving end of orders and commands and instructions? Yes, I do. And I'm sick of it."

"I don't blame you," Jacob said with a surprising degree of gentle understanding in his voice. "You do always seem to be at the bottom of the Ravenscroft pecking order. I guess it was too much of a temptation to resist letting your mother leap to a conclusion that was bound to upset her, wasn't it?"

Emily shrugged, afraid to point out again that her actions had been motivated as much by wanting to protect him as by annoyance. Jacob didn't seem to want protection. He probably thought he didn't need it. He just did not seem to comprehend how her family would react if they thought he was having an affair with Emily. He ought to know better, she thought, given the fact that he had worked for Ravenscrofts for years. Jacob, of all people, should know how ruthless the members of her family could be when they felt obliged to protect the company or one of their own.

Jacob's gaze turned affectionate as he watched Emily sitting in the middle of the bed, her arms hugging her knees. He came back across the room and tipped up her chin with one finger. Then he leaned down and kissed her lightly.

"Hey," he said softly, "it's going to be all right. You and I are starting something very good. We don't have to keep it a secret."

"I don't know, Jacob . . ."

"I do," he assured her with the limitless confidence of a man who has always been strong enough to get what he wanted and keep it. "You and I are lovers now and I want everyone, including your family, to know it."

"You know they won't approve, Jacob," she warned quietly.

"Let me worry about that. As of now, there's to be no more skulking around or misleading information given out concerning your love life."

"What am I supposed to do?" Emily asked waspishly. "Pass out announcements that I am now having an affair with you?"

"I think we can be a little more subtle than that."

"How?"

"I'll take you to your father's birthday party," Jacob said thoughtfully. "That should be as good a way as any of letting your family know how things stand between us."

Emily's eyes widened in shock. "You call that subtle?"

"I call it effective." He patted her on the top of the head and turned once more toward the bathroom. "See you in a few minutes. By the way, I'd like my eggs sunny-side up this morning and whole wheat toast."

The pillow Emily flung after him was a second too late. It struck the closed bathroom door instead of Jacob's head. She heard his pleased chuckle on the other side of the wall and then the sound of the shower drowned out the masculine laughter.

Emily sat for a long moment, contemplating the new direction her life had just taken. All the fierce protective feelings she had been experiencing earlier came back stronger than ever. Jacob might think he was invulnerable, but she knew her family a lot better than he did.

She knew in her heart that it was going to be up to her to provide the real protection for their relationship. She started to think seriously about ways of accomplishing that goal.

EMILY WAS still mulling over possible defenses later that morning as she fiddled with an experimental flower arrangement. This one involved some delicate freesia, a couple of irises and one magnificent lily.

"That's the ticket!" Diane exclaimed as she walked into the shop with the morning coffee. "A little more glitz and glamour. Now you're on the right track."

Emily gazed doubtfully down at her creation. "I don't know, Diane. It's too busy. It's not my style." She removed some of the freesia and instantly liked the new effect much better.

"I know, I know. You're the subtle type," Diane grumbled as she came around behind the counter. She peered at her friend. "Have an interesting evening?"

Emily looked up, startled by the unexpected question. "What's that supposed to mean?"

Diane smiled cagily. "Just a casual comment."

"Don't you dare ask about my love life."

"Why not?" Diane retorted innocently.

Emily grimaced. "Because at approximately 7:05 this morning my mother already did."

"What made her ask?"

"Guess," Emily said succinctly. She pulled out an iris, simplifying her creation further. Much better.

"Oh. So Mom called and realized you had a man with you at seven in the morning? Well, it was bound to happen sooner or later. Did you tell her who was with you?"

"No, I let her think it was Damon."

"Oh, Lord." Diane rolled her eyes ceilingward. "Does the hunk of granite know you fibbed about who was in bed with you?"

"Hunk of granite?"

"Sorry. That's how I think of Jacob Stone."

Emily sighed. "Yes, Jacob knows. He was furious."

"I'm not surprised."

"He doesn't seem to realize how upset my family will be if they find out I'm involved with him. I was only trying to protect him this morning when I allowed Mom to think Damon was there."

"I've got news for you, pal," Diane said darkly. "You don't protect a man like Jacob by pretending you're sleeping with someone else instead of him. Talk about stupid."

Emily spun around and folded her arms under her breasts. "All right, how do I go about protecting Jacob?"

"Not by substituting another man into the equation, that's for sure."

"What other approach is there?" Emily demanded, more of herself than of her friend. "I'm going to have to think of something and fast. Jacob is insisting on taking me to my father's birthday party on Thursday."

"He does believe in taking the bull by the horns, doesn't he?" Diane noted admiringly.

"Diane, this whole thing is going to explode on me. I know it is. I wanted a nice, quiet, private relationship with Jacob. But he won't allow it. He's too proud. Now I'm going to have to come up with a high-tech defense system in order to protect us."

"Any ideas?"

"Not yet," Emily admitted despairingly. "The only thing that ever really terrifies my family is a direct threat to Ravenscroft International. An attack from that direction is probably the only thing that would keep them in line, and how could I possibly threaten RI?"

"Beats me. Mind if I share that packet of sugar?"

Emily's fingers froze on the stem of the lily. The delicate stalk snapped in her hand. "Shares."

"What are you talking about?" Diane glanced at the broken flower.

"My shares in RI. They're mine, Diane."

"I know. So is the seat on the board of directors. What's that got to do with anything?"

Emily looked at her. "Theoretically I can do anything I want with those shares."

It was Diane's turn to stare as realization dawned. "Emily, you wouldn't dare use those shares to threaten your family."

"Why not?" Emily frowned, trying to think through the ramifications of such a daring plan.

"Are you kidding? From what you've told me about your family, I know enough to guess they would chew you up into little pieces if you tried a stunt like that. You'd never get away with it. They would never allow you to use those shares against them."

"They wouldn't have much choice in the matter." Emily spoke with sudden conviction. She yanked out the rest of the flowers in the arrangement and started from scratch, using a single crimson anthurium and three nearly bare branches.

"Emily, listen to me, this is crazy. You can't do it. You're not the type. Let Jacob handle your family."

"I can't take the risk," Emily said simply. "There's too much of a chance they'll find a way to drive him off. It's up to me to protect my relationship with Jacob."

Diane groaned. "I knew it. You really are in love, aren't you? The only other time I've seen you this determined to take a stand against your family was when you decided to open this shop."

"I survived that confrontation, didn't I?" Emily pointed out.

"Something tells me this scene is going to be a whole lot worse," Diane predicted gloomily.

6

MIDWAY THROUGH the gala social event that constituted Gifford Ravenscroft's birthday party, Jacob Stone looked around and discovered he was alone in the crowd. Emily had disappeared.

He swirled the Scotch in the glass he held in one hand. Ice cubes clinked. The small sound was barely audible in the laughter and chatter of the well-dressed guests. Jacob ran a quick, searching glance over the people standing nearby, but he didn't really expect to find Emily in their midst. He was not surprised when he didn't spot her.

He took a slow, meditative swallow of the Scotch and considered his next course of action. It was not hard to guess where he would eventually find Emily. By now she would have been taken aside by one or more Ravenscrofts and quietly asked to account for her choice of escorts to the annual family ball. Jacob decided he had better find her before she found herself cornered. She was a spirited little creature, but she was also very soft and vulnerable. He did not like the idea of her facing the wolf pack that was her family all by herself.

"Looking for someone, Stone?" A man of about fifty-five, portly and resplendent in formal black and white, glanced around as Jacob tried to ease his way through a cluster of businessmen.

"My date," Jacob explained ruefully. "I seem to have misplaced her. I turned my back for a moment and she vanished."

He recognized the man who had spoken to him. The name was Jensen. Jacob envied the man his easy air of elegance. Even though the older man was overweight and out of shape, Jensen looked at home in the tux. Jacob's evening suit was rented, and he was afraid it showed its origins. It wasn't that he couldn't afford to buy a tux, it was simply that he rarely ever needed one and saw no need to invest in clothes he would only wear once a year at the most. Emily hadn't seemed to mind his lack of interest in formal attire.

Ravenscroft International had once done Jensen a favor. Jacob had been the one sent out to dispense the favor in a suitably quiet manner. It had involved a small matter of industrial espionage. Jensen, a prominent Portland businessman, had not wanted to make any waves but he had needed discreet help. Gifford Ravenscroft had been happy to oblige and had supplied Jacob to do the job. Jensen had been suitably grateful to both RI and to Jacob.

"You're with Gifford's daughter, Emily, aren't you? I thought I saw her a few minutes ago," Jensen said helpfully, although his eyes were speculative. "She was with her brother."

"Thanks. I'll find her." Jacob started into the crowd. He was becoming very familiar with the kind of speculation he had seen in Jensen's gaze. That look had been in a lot of eyes tonight, including three sets of dark, brooding Ravenscroft eyes.

It had been apparent from the moment they walked into the paneled front hall of the Ravenscroft home that Emily had not bothered to tell her family in advance about Jacob Stone's new role in her life. At the time Jacob had not been sure if Emily's reticence had been due to nervousness or to her desire to shock her relatives. Whatever the reason, he had been mildly irritated. Several hours had passed, and he was still not sure why she had decided to spring their affair on her family without warning. He intended to pin her down about it after the party.

There had been a kind of gritty pride in the way Emily held her sleek head and in the straight line of her back as he had escorted her through the front door. Jacob had been both amused and proud even through his irritation. He knew what it took to confront a pack of Ravenscrofts. Emily had looked so cool and regal dressed in a long-sleeved, figure-hugging gown of dark turquoise silk. She had appeared totally unintimidated by her family but Jacob had felt the tension in her at the moment her mother had come forward to greet her.

There was no doubt but that everyone had been taken by surprise at the sight of Emily on Jacob's arm. Jacob had stood quietly by as she had greeted her family, assessing the quick astonishment and the cool appraisal that had flashed in the expressions of Drake, Catherine and Gifford.

Everyone had been polite and welcoming, of course. Gifford and Drake had greeted Jacob cheerfully and had offered their hands. Catherine had given him a small peck on the cheek and a warm smile. The Ravenscrofts might be ruthless on occasion, but they were nothing if not civilized on the surface. Jacob was not really certain how the Ravenscrofts had reacted to the knowledge that he was escorting their heretofore well-protected daughter. The truth was, he didn't really care.

But he did care about how Emily dealt with the situation, and he decided it was not a good idea to leave her alone with her family for very long. As he edged through the crowd, Jacob glanced at his watch. Emily had only been gone a few minutes. With any luck, not too much harm would have been done by the time he located her. She would probably welcome rescue by now.

Jacob smiled faintly at the thought.

THE DOOR to Gifford Ravenscroft's study closed silently behind Emily. It seemed to her there was something very ominous about that silence. It reminded her too much of the way the Ravenscrofts exercised their considerable power—quietly and with a great deal of finality. Drake, who had steered her into the room, dropped her arm and went to the teakwood bar at the far end of the study.

Emily steadied herself for the confrontation she knew was upon her. She had been mentally preparing for it since the morning Jacob had told her he intended to escort her to her father's party.

"Good heavens, Drake, we're alone. Where are Mom and Dad? I expected to have to face the entire assembled fleet, not just you." Her smile was bright and challenging as she made a pretense of strolling casually toward the window.

Her brother didn't glance up as he splashed whiskey into a glass. "I thought I'd talk to you first, Emily. I want to find out exactly what's going on between you and Jacob. You must have realized you gave Mom and Dad a real shock tonight when you sailed through the door on Stone's arm."

"What about you, Drake? Don't tell me you weren't a little surprised yourself."

Look what we've got for you:

Get 4 FREE full-length Harlequin Temptation® novels.

Plus
this handy compact manicure set

Plus
a surprise free gift

▼ PLUS LOTS MORE! MAIL THIS CARD TODAY ▼

Harlequin's Best-Ever "Get Acquainted" Offer

Yes, I'll try the Harlequin Reader Service under the terms outlined on the opposite page. Send me 4 free Harlequin Temptation® novels, a free compact manicure set and a free mystery gift.

142 CIH MDPF

PLACE STICKER
FOR 6 FREE GIFTS
HERE

NAME _____

ADDRESS _____ APT. _____

CITY _____

STATE _____ ZIP CODE _____

Gift offer limited to new subscribers, one per household. Terms and prices subject to change.

Don't forget...

...Return this card today to receive your 4 free books, free compact manicure set and free mystery gift.

...You will receive books before they're available in stores and at a discount off retail prices.

...No obligation. Keep only the books you want, cancel anytime.

If offer card is missing, write to: Harlequin Reader Service,
901 Fuhrmann Blvd., P.O. Box 1867, Buffalo, NY 14269-1867

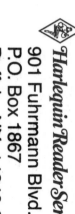

Drake appeared to consider that as he recapped the whiskey bottle. "Initially, but not now that I've had a chance to think about it. I should have guessed what was in the wind the night Stone insisted on driving you back to Seattle. Hell, I should have seen it coming when I first contacted him and asked him to find out everything he could about Morrell. It was obvious he was taking on the job for personal reasons, not just as a favor to RI."

"Is that right?" Emily asked dryly.

Drake shrugged one elegantly clad shoulder. "The trouble with Stone is that you can't often tell what he's thinking. He does things in his own way and in his own time and he does them for his own motives. I should have suspected that this time around the motivation was you. Even two years ago there was something about the way he used to look at you. But I didn't worry about it then. He was in the middle of a divorce and he was angry and bitter and heading abroad. I think he sensed that if he tried to get involved with you at that point in his life he would have savaged you. And you were too vulnerable yourself at that stage."

"I'm amazed you noticed anything at all about how I was feeling two years ago, Drake. I got the impression that all any of my family cared about was getting Brad Carlton out of my life, regardless of how I felt about the matter."

"Carlton was a weak, conniving worm. Getting him out of your life was priority number one. It had to be done before you were hurt any more than you already had been."

"You mean it had to be done before he had a chance to get his hands on a piece of Ravenscroft International," Emily corrected calmly.

Her brother gave her an odd glance. "You think the company is all the rest of us care about, don't you?"

"Oh, I think you're somewhat fond of me," Emily said with a trace of humor. "You're also overprotective, chauvinistic, paternalistic and irritating. I think, given half a chance, you and Mom and Dad would take over my life completely."

"We only want what's best for you, Em. You were always the baby in the family. And when you did grow up you didn't turn out to be quite what Mom and Dad had expected." It was Drake's turn to look amused. "They don't understand you."

"And you do?"

"Not completely. I'll admit you're different in some ways from the rest of us. But I think I've got a better understanding of you than Mom and Dad ever will. That doesn't mean they don't love you."

Emily sighed. "I know. If I didn't believe that, I wouldn't put up with them at all, you know."

"Stone has made himself your lover, hasn't he?"

Emily blinked rapidly at the unexpected question. Then her mouth tilted wryly. Drake was using a familiar Ravenscroft interrogation technique. "That's a Ravenscroft for you. Distract the victim with pleasant chatter about family affection and then, when her defenses are down, zing her with the real question." She moved aside the window drape and gazed out into the lighted garden. "My relationship with Jacob is a personal matter. I see no need to discuss it."

"No games, Em. Just tell me the truth. I might be able to help you."

Emily glanced suspiciously over her shoulder. "Help me? How?"

Drake lounged on his father's heavy wood desk and gave his sister an affectionate glance. "You know what I'm talking about. I can handle Mom and Dad a lot better than you can. I understand them. Especially Dad."

"Because you're a lot like him?"

Drake shrugged. "Maybe. That's not the point. The point is that Mom and Dad aren't exactly thrilled with the idea of you sleeping with Jacob Stone."

"What makes them think I am?"

"They're not fools, Em," Drake said impatiently. "We all saw the look in his eyes when he walked through the door with you. Possessive as hell. The man was staking a claim and daring us to challenge it."

"Here you all were wasting precious time worrying about my relationship with Morrell while the real threat moved in undetected. An extremely rare case of a bunch of Ravenscrofts caught off guard. How do you feel about the whole thing, big brother?"

"I won't say I'm thrilled about it." Drake took a sip of his whiskey. "You're my kid sister. You've been my kid sister since the day you were born and you'll still be my kid sister thirty years from now. I'm probably not ever going to like the idea of any man having an affair with you. Part of me wants to protect you from the wicked ways of my own species. Dad and Mom, of course, being parents, feel even more strongly about it. But I'm willing to admit that we've interfered in your life too many times in the past. Maybe it's time you got to make your own decisions."

Emily turned completely around to face him. She folded her arms, aware that she was so keyed up that she was almost trembling. She took three slow breaths to calm herself. "Translated, I gather that means you think that if I'm determined to have an affair it might as well be with someone you think you can control. Someone such as Jacob."

Drake's eyes narrowed. "I didn't say that. And it's not what I meant. I like Jacob. You know that."

"But you don't think he's good enough to be my lover?"

Drake met her eyes. "I think," he said slowly, "that Stone is dangerous. He lives up to his name, Emily. You've never really seen the hard, tough side of him. I have. Believe me, if you think we Ravenscrofts are ruthless at times, you should see Jacob Stone when he goes after something he wants."

"You're trying to scare me off, aren't you, Drake?"

"I'm not trying to frighten you, I'm trying to give you a few facts."

Before Emily could respond to that remark, the study door opened again to admit Catherine and Gifford Ravenscroft. They walked into the room with serious, intent expressions, their eyes going instantly to their daughter.

"Ah," said Emily, "Reinforcements have arrived. You're not alone any longer, Drake. Mom and Dad are here to explain to me in great detail why I should get Jacob out of my life."

"You don't have to act as if we represent the Inquisition. We all like Jacob," Gifford said coolly as he closed the door behind himself and his wife. "I'd trust him with my life."

"But not with your daughter?" Emily asked.

Catherine sat down in one of the wing chairs, the skirts of her peach-colored silk dress swirling gracefully. "Now, dear, you must know how startled we all were to find out you're, uh, dating Jacob. Why didn't you say something on the phone the other morning? It was Jacob who was with you, wasn't it?"

"I didn't feel like talking about my private affairs the other morning and I don't feel like it now. My love life is no one's business." Emily eyed the members of her family, gathering her nerve. What she was about to do was going to require all her courage and fortitude.

"Emily, there's no need to be rude to your mother. You've given us all a shock this evening and I think you know it." Gifford shoved one hand into his pocket and walked over to the teak bar to pour himself a drink. "We had no idea you and Jacob were interested in each other."

"If we had," Catherine murmured regretfully, "we would have handled things differently a couple of weeks ago when we asked him for help in dealing with Morrell. Jacob's not the right man for you, Emily. I don't even understand why you're interested in him."

Feeling besieged, Emily held her ground by the window. The forces of Ravenscroft disapproval were gathering around her. Soon she would be in the center of a whirlwind. She had to keep her head as her family marshaled its assault.

"I'm the one who's surprised," she said mockingly. "I thought you all liked and trusted Jacob. I assumed you'd all be delighted that I'd finally started dating someone you approved of."

Catherine sighed. "Don't be deliberately dense, Emily, dear. We are very fond of Jacob and, as your father says, we trust him. We've trusted him with Ravenscroft secrets for years. That's not the point."

"What is the point?" Emily challenged softly.

Catherine waved her hand in a graceful, vague gesture. "Well, dear, to tell you the truth, although Jacob has always been quite useful and loyal to RI, he's not quite what we had in mind for you. His background is, well, murky, to say the least. He's led a rather rough-and-ready life, you know. Quite a different background than your own. Then, too, there was that nasty business at the time of his divorce . . ."

"I'm not marrying him, Mother. Jacob made it clear a long time ago he's not interested in marriage. You don't have to worry about having him for a son-in-law, if that's what's troubling you."

She could not have made it any clearer that she was involved in an affair, Emily thought. But perhaps if she defused their fears of her marrying Jacob right at the beginning, she could gain an edge. As she scanned the faces of the other three, she realized they were not exactly reassured. In fact, they all appeared more concerned than ever.

"Emily," Catherine tried again, "Jacob has many fine qualities, but he's not exactly your type. It would be kinder not to encourage him."

"What is my type, Mother?"

Gifford frowned forbiddingly at his daughter's tone. "You know what your mother is trying to say. Jacob comes from an entirely different background than you do. He grew up the hard way and it shows. He's got some rough edges, and you'll never succeed in polishing him to the point where he'll fit into the sort of crowd we have here tonight."

"You've found some of his rough edges very useful in the past, haven't you?" Emily asked bluntly. "You've used them to cut a path for RI when more polite and civilized techniques didn't succeed in getting you what you want."

"A firm such as ours occasionally has need of the kind of talents Jacob has," Gifford admitted calmly. "That doesn't mean I want him sleeping with my daughter."

Catherine winced at the blunt words, but she nodded her head in agreement. "Jacob's simply not the right man for you, Emily. I suppose you think he's romantic or something, but the truth is you only got involved with him on the rebound. You were angry about the way we handled the Morrell situation, and when Jacob offered you an alternative, you apparently fell into his arms. I can understand how it happened. But your father and I have decided it would be best if you put a stop to your relationship with him. There's no future in it, and you'll only wind up getting hurt."

The study door opened on silent hinges just as Emily's mother finished speaking. Jacob stood on the threshold, assessing the small group with cold eyes. Then he folded his arms and leaned against the doorjamb. There was no doubt but that he had heard Catherine's last words. But he said nothing, merely waited for Emily to react to her mother's unsubtle command.

Emily felt a rush of glorious power pouring through her. This was the moment she had been waiting for, and it was satisfying that Jacob would be here to witness it. Too bad Grandmother Ravenscroft wasn't present. Emily had a hunch the old woman would have enjoyed herself. Emily faced her family triumphantly.

"I will say this one more time. My relationship with Jacob is my own business. I won't tolerate any more interference in my life from any of you. I have had enough."

Gifford and Catherine Ravenscroft scowled, first at Jacob and then at their daughter. Drake quietly sipped his whiskey and watched the small drama being played out in front of him as if he found the whole thing suddenly amusing.

It was Catherine who tried to take charge of the situation. "I think this can be discussed some other time.

Gifford, we should get back to our guests." She rose to her feet.

Gifford moved to take her arm, his unreadable gaze sweeping over Jacob. "I think you're right, my dear. Emily, we'll talk later."

"No," said Emily. "We'll talk now. I have something to say. I will keep it short."

"It can wait, dear," her mother began warningly.

Emily ignored her. "You will all do me the courtesy of listening to what I have to say. As it concerns the future of Ravenscroft International, I'm sure you'll want to hear it."

Drake, Gifford and Catherine froze, their eyes suddenly riveted on Emily.

"Good," Emily said with satisfaction. "I finally have your attention. Nothing like mentioning RI to make sure everyone's listening to me."

"What are you talking about, Emily?" Drake asked coolly.

She braced herself, aware of Jacob watching her. This was the moment she had been preparing for all evening. She had to play this right if she was going to succeed in protecting him. "It's quite simple. I've decided I've had enough family interference in my life. I am demanding that all of you stay out of my way from here on out. To ensure some peace and quiet for myself, I am going to give you all an ultimatum."

"Emily, don't be ridiculous," Catherine said uneasily. She stopped talking, apparently unable to think of anything else to say. The men just stared at Emily.

Jacob was very still in the doorway. Emily could not begin to read his mood, but that did not seem terribly important at the moment. She was riding high on her own strength and independence. For the first time in her life she was about to use a Ravenscroft tactic.

"I know how you people work," Emily said, savoring the moment. "I've watched you for years and on occasion I've been the victim of some of your Machiavellian methods. I think I've finally learned some of the techniques. Pay attention because this is the bargain I'm going to make with you. I will give you my word of honor to let you continue voting my shares in RI as you see fit as long as you stay out of my life and as long as you leave Jacob alone."

"Dammit, Emily, what the hell are you saying?" Gifford snapped furiously. His expression was one of outrage and astonishment. He would have started toward his daughter, but his wife caught hold of his arm.

"You heard me," Emily stated firmly. "If any one of you tries to manipulate Jacob, if you try to interfere in my relationship with him, I will start looking for a buyer for my RI shares. I'm sure I could turn up several interested parties on short notice. Damon Morrell would no doubt be at the head of the line."

Drake was shaking his head ruefully. "Oh, Emily," he muttered.

"I can't believe I'm hearing this," Gifford thundered at his daughter. "You wouldn't dare do such a thing. Are you out of your mind, girl?"

"No, I'm finally taking charge of my own life." Emily walked across an Oriental carpet toward the door, her eyes fastened on Jacob's face. "It's about time, don't you think?"

"You can't mean that," Catherine whispered in a stricken voice.

Emily turned to glance at her mother. "Oh, but I do. If you try to use any means of coercing him, I swear I will sell my shares within twenty-four hours."

Her parents appeared frozen.

Drake watched his sister for a moment, and then his attention switched to Jacob's implacable expression. "Emily seems to have made her choice tonight. Treat her well, Stone, or I'll carve you up with a dull knife."

Jacob straightened away from the door and reached out to take Emily's arm. He looked at Drake. "I guess we all should have remembered that underneath the softness, she's still a Ravenscroft. I could have told you it was dangerous to push any Ravenscroft into a corner. Don't worry, Drake. She's in good hands."

Emily's pulse was racing with the adrenaline of victory as Jacob led her down the deserted hallway. Her step was light and full of energy. She almost laughed with exuberance.

"I did it," she sang out softly. "I did it. I stood up to them and made them all back off. It was even better this time than it was when I got my own loan for my shop because this time I used their own tactics. I finally beat them at their own game."

"You threw them for a loop, I'll give you that." Jacob piloted her toward the rear of the house. "I hope you enjoyed it."

"I did. Oh, Jacob, it was wonderful. It was a fantastic sensation. I should have started using those shares a long time ago to keep them out of my hair. I don't know why I didn't think of it before now. I feel like I'm finally free. I faced them down. I won. *I won.*"

"You think so?" Jacob asked cryptically.

It finally dawned on Emily that he was not sharing her jubilation. She frowned slightly, forced to quicken her steps to keep up with him. He was pacing along the hall with the long, smooth stride of a leopard on the prowl. "Of course I did. You saw them. They were all dumbfounded by my threat. They care more about those shares than they do about anything else in the world."

"I think you underestimate your family, Emily."

They had reached a door that opened onto a back garden. Jacob turned the knob with a fiercely controlled movement and pulled Emily outside into the chilly, damp night. Emily finally became aware of her surroundings.

"What are we doing out here? Where are we going?"

"I'm taking you to a hotel near the airport where you can spend the night and tomorrow morning I'm putting you on a plane to Seattle."

"A hotel? But, Jacob, the evening isn't over. I don't want to leave just yet."

"I know. You want to hang around and enjoy your little victory, don't you? But I'm not in the mood to indulge you tonight, Emily. I've had enough Ravenscroft drama for one evening."

Emily was totally bewildered. "Jacob, I don't understand this. What's going on? Are you afraid to stay at the party? You don't have to worry about my family anymore. I've got them under control at last."

"I'm not worried about your family. I never was worried about them. I told you that several days ago." Jacob fished a set of keys out of his pocket as he led Emily down the path to where his car was parked.

"But, Jacob, you don't understand. My family would have made our lives hell. I had to make it clear to them that this time I would not tolerate any interference. I conducted that little scene in the study to protect you."

"The hell you did. You did it because you've been looking for a way to punish your family for the way they handled the situation between you and Damon Morrell. You've probably wanted to pay them back in their own coin for years because of what you call their interference in your life. Tonight you found a way, didn't you?"

Emily was truly alarmed. "Jacob, that's not how it was." He cut off the rest of her protest by the simple expedient of settling her in the car seat and closing the door.

"You used me," Jacob said quietly as he opened his own door and got behind the wheel. "You used me to retaliate against your family."

Emily stared at him, trying to read his mood in the hard lines of his face. It was slowly sinking in that Jacob was coldly furious.

"That's not true," she whispered.

"Sure it is." He started the engine and eased the car out of the driveway. "You learned a lot from that assertiveness training, didn't you? Including strategy. As a Ravenscroft you're something of a late bloomer, but you finally showed you've got some of the family talent. You wanted a showdown and you created it. Those shares in RI constituted the weapon you'd been looking for. Protecting me was your excuse for using it."

"It wasn't an excuse! Jacob, I did it for you."

"Don't hand me that line. I don't recall asking for protection."

Emily was suddenly incensed. She had been through a lot this evening and to learn that Jacob did not appreciate anything she had done was too much. Didn't he realize the jeopardy they had been in? "Why don't you believe me when I tell you I did it for you? For years I've been expected to put up with all sorts of interference in my life on the grounds that people were just doing it for my own good. You yourself have fed me that line on more than one occasion. What's so illogical about my acting out of similar motives? What I just did, I did for your own good."

He shot her a swift, savage glance. It was a look that revealed far too much about his current mood. Emily remembered what Drake had said about Jacob's being potentially dangerous. She watched him, wide-eyed, and withdrew as far as she could into the corner of her seat.

"I know what was motivating you tonight, little witch. I should have guessed several days ago just why you surrendered to me so easily."

Emily gasped. "Don't you dare call my going to bed with you an act of surrender."

"You're right. It wasn't an act of sweet, feminine surrender at all, was it? It was a tactical move. I'll have to hand it to you, Emily. Up until that scene in the study I didn't realize what you had in mind. I knew you were tense and that you seemed to be nerving yourself up for something, but I thought you were just worried about what your family would think when they saw you with me."

"That was exactly what I was worried about."

He shook his head. "No. You were working yourself up for your big victory assault. You had decided you could use me as a means of demonstrating your independence to your family. You knew you couldn't use Morrell because doing so would have meant the risk of doing serious damage to RI and to your relatives. Morrell would have found a way to use you to wreck RI. Deep down, you're a Ravenscroft, too, and the last thing you would do is cause real irreparable harm to the company. But you figured it was safe to use me because fundamentally I'm loyal to the firm. You knew you could trust me to never actually try to take control of your chunk of RI. You could taunt your family with our affair and threaten to sell the shares if they didn't stay out of your life because you thought it was safe for you to use me. Unlike Morrell, I don't represent a real risk to RI."

Emily was appalled. Her whole world seemed to be turning upside down. She turned her head to gaze blindly out the window. "I can't believe you're interpreting things this way," she whispered dully. "I just can't believe it. I only did it to protect you."

"Whatever made you think I needed protection?" he asked coldly. "What the hell did you think your family could do to me?"

Emily hugged her arms around herself. She suddenly felt sick. "I thought my family might try to manipulate you. I wanted them to know they couldn't get away with it. I just went through the biggest showdown of my life with my family for your sake."

Jacob concentrated his attention on the traffic. "You went through that showdown because you've been looking for revenge. You've probably dreamed of it for years. You finally put nerve, opportunity and means together to get it. You should have seen the look on your face when you knew you had won."

Emily frantically tried one last time to explain. "I was happy because I thought I had just managed to protect you and our...our relationship."

"You were thrilled because you had finally beaten your family at their own game. I have to hand it to you, Emily. You looked and acted like a real Ravenscroft back there in the study."

Emily swallowed miserably, fighting tears. "And you don't want a real Ravenscroft in your bed, is that it? You want sweet, pliable little Emily who can't handle her own life and who needs someone around to tell her what to do. You want the Emily who *surrenders* when you make love to her. You want the old Emily. I'm not her, Jacob. I've changed. I guess you hadn't realized that until tonight."

"You're wrong," Jacob said as he parked in front of a large downtown hotel near the river. "I want the strong new Emily who isn't intimidated by her family or anyone else. I want the Emily who has built a business for herself without her family's help. I want the Emily who has the courage to become involved in an affair with me even though she knows her family won't approve. But I won't let that new Emily use me the way she did tonight."

Torn between fury and despair, Emily choked on useless words as Jacob removed her small overnight case from the trunk of his car and escorted her into the hotel. She continued to say nothing as he booked a room for her at the front desk and walked her to the elevators. When he deposited her in front of a door, her overbright eyes met his, her lashes glistening with tears. She knew he was not going to stay with her.

"So this is how it ends?" she asked, her nails digging into her palms as she fought for composure. This was so much worse than the night he had put her in a cab after kissing her to the point of abandon.

But Emily refused to cry in front of him. She had her pride. It was all she had left, and she was grimly determined to hang on to it. The old Emily would have been in tears by now.

Jacob watched her with a hooded gaze. He was hard, implacable, immovable. A tough, dangerous man, just as Drake had warned.

"No," Jacob said calmly, "this is not how it ends. With any luck, someday we'll look back on this moment as a beginning."

Emily was suddenly excruciatingly weary. "I don't understand."

He framed her face with his strong hands. "Try thinking about it, Emily, instead of reacting with raw emotion. Try to get past that damned Ravenscroft pride of yours and think about what you did to me tonight. I've got my pride, too, you know. I don't need your protection, and I will not tolerate being used, not even by you. You had no right to pull that stunt in your father's study this evening."

Anger and confusion welled up within her. "What do you want from me?" she said.

"An apology."

"An apology!"

"For a start," he confirmed.

"Never!" Emily exploded as fury overwhelmed all the other emotions in a white-hot, cleansing fire. "I don't have anything to apologize for. What I did, I did for your sake. I was not using you to take my revenge, dammit."

"And after you've apologized," Jacob continued, ignoring her heartfelt protest, "you and I are going to sit down and have a long, calm discussion about the ground rules for this affair of ours."

"Why, you overbearing, conceited, arrogant bastard. Who do you think you are?"

His eyes flared but he didn't respond to the wild, emotional accusation. "When we're done with that discussion we'll have a little talk about the future. Good night, Emily. Call me when you're ready to admit you used me tonight to carry out a personal vendetta against your family. When you're ready to give me your word of honor you won't ever try a stunt like that again, we'll work out the rest of this relationship."

Dazed with shock and anger Emily stared after Jacob as he turned away and walked down the corridor to the elevators. Within seconds he was gone.

7

SHE'D HAD THE NERVE to claim she had been trying to protect him. Jacob did not know which infuriated him most—having Emily use him and her RI shares to threaten her family, or having her claim afterward that she had only done it to protect him from Ravenscroft wrath.

He could not believe she had actually thought he needed protecting, so he dismissed her claim out of hand. That meant his initial analysis had to have been right. She had finally taken her stand against her family in a big way, and Jacob found himself being used as a pawn.

It was the only logical explanation, he told himself over and over again. She could not possibly have been so witless as to actually think she had to do something that dramatic to protect him.

Could she?

Several hours later, at two in the morning to be exact, Jacob was awake, pacing the living room of his apartment and agonizing over the way he had handled Emily's bold act of assertiveness.

It was unlike him to agonize over any decision, and Jacob was as furious with himself for his own uneasiness as he had been earlier with Emily.

He stalked barefoot into the kitchen and reached into a cupboard for a bottle of medicinal Scotch. It was going to be a long night, and the knowledge that Emily was spending it not more than a couple of miles away in a lonely hotel room did not make things any easier.

He had to stand firm on this, Jacob reminded himself for the thousandth time as he splashed a healthy swallow of Scotch into a water glass. He was not normally a tolerant man, but he had long ago realized he would probably tolerate almost anything from Emily. Still, he had to draw some lines with her.

Dammit, he wanted her to want him for himself, not because she had decided he was strong enough to be used in a power play against her family.

Jacob tossed back the Scotch and prowled restlessly back out into the living room. From his window he could see the lights of the hotel where Emily was staying. It was torture to stand here thinking about how good it would be to spend the night in Emily's bed. Self-inflicted torture. He must be turning into some sort of stupid masochist.

But it would be even more masochistic to let her turn him into a club that she could use to beat the other Ravenscrofts over the head.

It was obvious to Jacob that in the past couple of years Emily had finally begun to tap into her own strength as a woman and as a Ravenscroft. Until tonight he had been glad to see the transformation, aware that she had come into her own and aware, too, that on some level she was free to love him now.

But tonight Jacob had been shattered to discover that her motives for becoming involved with him were not the simple, straightforward result of womanly passion.

He did not doubt the passion. That had been real enough. His body tightened at the memory of Emily flowering in his arms. But tonight he had realized that she might have come to him for more subtle and complex reasons. He was worried now that she had fallen so easily into his arms because she had sensed instinctively that he was the one man she could use to retaliate against her family for years of overprotectiveness and interference.

He'd give a great deal to get his hands on that damned assertiveness training course instructor. Whoever he or she was, that person had done the job of bringing Emily out of her shell only too well. Of course, the instructor had had basic Ravenscroft material—tempered steel—with which to work, Jacob reminded himself wryly.

Jacob stared out the window at the lights of the hotel. He wanted Emily more than he had ever wanted anything else in his life. God knew he had waited long enough for her. But he wanted her to love him for himself, not because she could use him to finally take a stand against her family.

Jacob swore silently as he examined the web in which he was caught. He, of all people, should have realized how dangerous it was to get involved with Ravenscrofts. Corner any one of them, even the youngest and the softest little female in the bunch, and you found out fast enough they all had claws.

Jacob grinned reluctantly. He wouldn't deny Emily the right to unsheath those claws once in a while. He was too much of a predator himself not to understand her need to fight back occasionally. Hell, he needed a woman who could hold her own. He had no use for wimps, male or female.

He glanced at his watch and promised himself he would see Emily first thing in the morning. He was convinced that all she needed was a little time to think. By breakfast she would have had the whole night to reconsider her actions. Jacob was sure she would realize that she had been wrong to confuse her feelings for him with her need to take a stand against her family.

It would be worth the lonely wait tonight to give her time to sort things out. She was an intelligent woman. What's more, she was falling in love with him, Jacob told himself. That love was his high card. She might be a Ravenscroft, but she was different from the others. She was too gentle to dig in her heels over this, for instance.

All he had to do was give her a little time. When she was ready to admit she had been wrong, he would be ready and waiting to graciously accept her apology.

But at seven o'clock the next morning when Jacob knocked on her hotel door prepared for tearful remorse, he was stunned to discover that Emily had already left Portland. She had caught an early-morning plane back to Seattle.

At first he couldn't believe she had fled. She was too honest, too sweet and too much at the mercy of her own gentle conscience not to stick around and apologize for what she had done.

She was acting as if she were the one who had been abused, he thought furiously.

That chilled him. If she truly felt wronged it could only be because she actually had faced her family for his sake.

Jacob drove back to his apartment grimly wondering for the first time if he might have misjudged Emily's motives for staging the scene in her father's study.

She was just naïve enough still to think he might need protection. And she was just reckless enough to try to offer the only defense she thought she could provide.

"EMILY, YOU'RE GOING TO RUIN our whole inventory of tulips if you keep jamming them into your arrangement like that." Diane glowered at her boss as Emily tossed another broken tulip into a nearby trash bin.

"I haven't got much time to come up with a decent design," Emily muttered as she eyed her bedraggled creation. "The show is tonight. If I'm going to enter, I have to get my arrangement in by five o'clock this afternoon."

"I know that, but you aren't going to create anything brilliant by attacking the poor flowers. What's the matter with you, anyway? You've been acting weird since you got back from Portland yesterday. Did you and Jacob quarrel?"

"It's none of your business." Emily picked up another tulip and scanned her latest arrangement like a general preparing for battle.

"Aha, so you did have a fight. I knew it." Diane broke off abruptly as the shop door opened and a customer ambled inside. She helped the woman choose some cut flowers, wrapped them for her and collected the money. When the shop door closed behind the customer, Diane turned to her friend as if there had been no break in the discussion. "So tell me about it."

"There's nothing to tell," Emily said tightly. "I made another mistake. I tend to do that a lot when it comes to judging men. Have you noticed?"

"Emily, stop feeling sorry for yourself and tell me what happened in Portland."

Emily chewed on her lower lip while she considered her answer. She discovered she wanted to talk to a friend. The crushing weight of the disaster was becoming too much for her. She tossed a tulip down on the counter and looked at her assistant.

"I only wanted to protect him, Diane."

"Protect Jacob? From what?"

"My family."

Diane nodded wisely. "Uh-oh."

"I was getting the usual static from my parents and from Drake," Emily explained. "Yes, they trust Jacob, but no, they don't think he's the kind of man I should get involved with. Yes, they like Jacob, but no, he's not right for me. Not the right social background. Divorced. Too hard. Too dangerous. I'll only get hurt. And so on."

"So what did you do?"

Emily looked down at her hands. "I tried to run a bluff."

"How?"

Emily sighed. "I told them that if they tried to manipulate Jacob into leaving me alone, I would sell my shares in Ravenscroft International to the first buyer who came along. Jacob walked into the room just as I was making my grand stand."

"Oh, my God." Diane groaned and collapsed back against the counter.

"I made a major tactical error," Emily said grimly. "Jacob instantly jumped to the conclusion that I was conducting my big scene in order to retaliate against my parents. He thought I was using him and my shares in RI to get even with them for all their interference in my life."

"I gather he took exception to the way you handled the big confrontation?"

"He was furious," Emily said quietly. "He refused to listen when I tried to explain that I had only done it to protect him."

"Of course he did, you idiot. What man wants to think he needs protection, or worse, that his woman thinks she has to protect him?"

Emily closed her eyes in silent misery. "I guess I really blew it, didn't I?"

"Sounds like it," Diane agreed rather heartlessly. But there was an underlying sympathy in her voice when she added soothingly, "I have a hunch it will all work itself out in the end, though."

"What makes you think that?"

"Simple. Jacob wants you too much to let this situation go on very long. And you want him. You're in love with the man, Emily. Admit it."

"I'm in love with him." It wasn't hard to admit. She had known it on one level or another for almost five years. The knowledge was a part of her now. "But, Diane, he doesn't realize the danger he's in. He does need protection from my family, whether he wants to acknowledge it or not. They don't want him involved with me, and they'll find a way to get rid of him if I don't use those shares as a real threat. My stake in RI is all I have with which to control them."

"How can your family put pressure on him to get him to leave you alone?"

"They'll find a way," Emily predicted morosely. "It might be something very subtle, such as suggesting to him that he's no good for me and that if he cares for me he'll exit, stage right."

"Hmm. Interesting approach. Think Jacob would fall for it?"

"He might, if it was handled cleverly enough. After all, Jacob has a deep sense of loyalty to Ravenscrofts in general and to my father in particular. If Dad went to him and told him he should sacrifice his relationship with me for my sake, it's possible Jacob would believe him. Or Dad might try another tactic. Who knows? That's the whole problem."

"So you thought you'd short-circuit your family by making it clear you'd dump the shares in RI if they made any kind of move to get rid of Jacob." Diane hesitated. "You know something, Emily, that was pretty gutsy of you. There must have been a nuclear explosion after you delivered your ultimatum."

"I don't know. Jacob rushed me away before I had a chance to see how my family took the blackmail. They aren't accustomed to me taking a firm stand with them, though. The only other occasions I've really stood up to them were when they refused to give me a loan for this shop and when they wanted me to surrender my seat on the RI board of directors."

"You know something, Emily?" Diane murmured. "I've always kind of wondered why you didn't give up that seat. You're not really interested in RI. Why did you take a stand on that issue?"

Emily shrugged. "I had no choice. I made a promise."

"To yourself?"

Emily shook her head quickly. "No. To Grandmother. That's not important now. The important thing is, what am I going to do about the disaster I've created with Jacob?"

"I give up. What are you going to do?"

"I don't know." Emily fiddled with some vines she frequently used as backdrop greenery for her arrangements. "I just don't know. Maybe this is the end of it. I haven't heard from Jacob since I left yesterday morning."

"Be fair, Emily. He hasn't heard from you, either."

"He wants an apology for the way he thinks I used him."

"Are you going to apologize?"

"Diane, I didn't use him! I was trying to protect him. If he can't realize that, what hope is there for any kind of real relationship between us?"

"What hope is there for any kind of real relationship if you don't start communicating with him?" Diane asked reasonably.

A wave of despair and panic washed over Emily. "You're right, I guess."

"You're dealing with a man's ego here, Emily. That is not one of nature's more rational creations."

"Why do women always have to be the reasonable, rational ones? It's not fair," Emily protested, knowing now she was fighting a losing battle. She'd lost enough battles in her life to recognize the signs.

"Nature is not always inclined to play fair."

Emily picked up a handful of flowers. "Right again. I might as well bite the bullet and apologize, even though I have absolutely nothing to apologize for. You know, Diane, this really goes against the grain."

Diane laughed. "Spoken like a true Ravenscroft. Never give an inch."

"I wasn't planning on giving inches. I think I'll send the traditional apology."

"What's that?"

Emily smiled wryly and held up a rose. "The problem is," she said sadly, "even if he accepts the apology, we're still back to square one. Since he won't let me blackmail my family with those shares, I have no other way to protect our relationship. My family will start trying to wear us down as soon as they know the shares are safe. How long can a love affair last under those circumstances?"

"You won't know until you try. First step is sending the roses."

THE TWO DOZEN YELLOW ROSES arrived just as Jacob was throwing the last pair of jockey shorts into his overnight bag. He answered the doorbell impatiently, intent only on getting rid of whoever stood on the other side. It was going to be a long drive to Seattle and he wanted to get going.

The sight of the floral delivery boy left Jacob briefly openmouthed with astonishment.

"You must have the wrong apartment." He started to close the door.

"No, wait—it says Stone, apartment number 1202," the young man said quickly. "This is 1202, isn't it? Isn't your name Stone?"

"Yeah, but I didn't order any flowers."

"These are for you," the boy insisted. "Here. Take them." He grinned suddenly. "You don't have to look so shocked. More and more women are sending flowers to men these days. I know it's kind of mushy, but that's how females are."

Jacob's brows came together in a hard line as he frowned down at the box of flowers. "They're from a woman?"

"Yup. That's what my boss said. There's a card attached. What's the matter? Don't you know any woman who might want to send you a couple dozen roses?"

A rush of exuberant pleasure went through Jacob. He reached out and snatched the box out of the boy's hands. "Let me have those. Thanks. Here, this is for you." He fished hurriedly through his wallet for a five-dollar bill.

"Geez, thanks, mister," the boy said, clearly stunned by the size of the tip.

"Forget it. I was in the delivery business once myself."

Jacob closed the apartment door, the box of roses cradled carefully in one arm and walked slowly into the kitchen. He had never received flowers in his life, and he tried to think of what to do first.

"Water," he muttered with sudden insight. "They have to go into water."

He put the box down on a counter and started opening cupboards. Belatedly he remembered he did not own a flower vase. After going through three cupboards, he realized he did not own anything that even resembled a vase. No jars, no pitchers, not even a small bucket. He looked around the kitchen, drumming his fingers impatiently on the sink.

Then he remembered the bottle of Scotch he had nearly drained the night he'd left Emily at the hotel.

Jacob snatched the bottle out of the closet and carelessly poured what remained of the expensive liquor into a large glass. Then he rinsed out the bottle and set it back down on the counter. Very carefully, handling the roses as if they were newborn kittens, he began inserting them into the empty Scotch bottle.

He managed to get three stems into the narrow neck of the bottle. Jacob added water and then began searching for other containers for the roses. There was a half-empty mayonnaise jar in the refrigerator, he discovered.

"Who needs mayonnaise?" he asked himself aloud. "The stuff isn't good for you, anyway." He dumped the mayonnaise down the garbage disposal and washed out the jar. After that he got increasingly creative.

Fifteen minutes later he dried his hands on a paper towel and examined his collection of floral designs. They certainly weren't up to Emily's standards, but he was rather pleased with the effect. Two dozen yellow roses adorned the kitchen, occupying the empty Scotch bottle, the mayonnaise jar, a plastic milk carton and a salad dressing bottle. The place looked like a garden to Jacob.

All his flower garden lacked was the sweet Ravens-croft witch who touched him with magic whenever she was nearby. He took the little card out of its envelope and reread it. The message was short and to the point: "I apologize. Emily." But Jacob felt an odd rush of emotion each time he read the note.

She wouldn't have sent the flowers and the note if she had not decided her affair with him was more important than her Ravenscroft pride. Tonight he would tell her that his own pride had been less important to him than his relationship with her. He was feeling magnanimous and incredibly relieved. He would tell her that he had been packing to go to her even before the flowers arrived.

Jacob took one last, satisfied look at his yellow roses and then went back to his packing. With a little luck he would be in Seattle in time to attend Emily's flower show this evening.

BUT LUCK was in short supply on the interstate outside Seattle. A four-car pileup brought everything to a standstill for nearly an hour. By the time the freeway cleared, Jacob knew there was no point in trying to get to the flower show. It was far too late. He decided to head straight for Emily's downtown apartment.

He used the garage access card she had given him to open the steel gates of the underground parking facility, glancing at his watch as he did so. She should be arriving home herself very soon. He wondered how she would react when she found him waiting for her. Then he scowled as he glanced around at the shadowed, empty garage. He definitely did not like the idea of Emily coming and going from this place on a regular basis. Women in the city had to exercise extra precautions.

As the gates closed behind him, Jacob guided his car into an empty slot, switched off the ignition and climbed out. He went around to the trunk to get his overnight bag.

Jacob had his bag in one hand and his other hand on the trunk lid when he realized he was not alone in the garage. He swung around, instinctively dropping into a slight crouch.

There were two of them. Young, male and vicious. They were wearing jeans, black jackets and dirty sport shoes. They came from between a pair of parked cars on the opposite side of the garage, moving fast. One of them carried a length of metal pipe and the other wielded a knife.

It could have been worse, Jacob had time to reflect. They might have had guns.

Then there wasn't any more time to think about it. There was only time to react and barely enough at that.

The one with the metal pipe reached him first, moving in low and bringing the pipe down in a short, violent arc. Jacob blocked the blow with his overnight bag and then crowded in behind it before the attacker could raise the pipe again. He used his foot to aim a crippling blow at the man's kneecap. His assailant yelled, dropped the pipe and clutched wildly at his injured knee.

"Get him, for Christ's sake! *Get him!*" the man screamed at his partner.

Jacob twisted as the other man launched himself forward, knife in hand. He dodged the first quick rush and managed to bring the heel of his palm down across the back of the assailant's neck. The man gasped and sprawled forward into the trunk. Jacob slammed the lid and held it down, pinning the knife-wielding arm in the metal jaws of the trunk until the knife fell to the concrete floor.

Jacob turned to check the status of the other punk and caught the full impact of a fist on the side of his jaw. The attacker followed it up with a body blow and a kick in the ribs.

Pain exploded, almost immediately swamped by cold fury. Jacob reeled back, releasing the trunk. When the younger man closed in on him, Jacob let him get very close before he made his move.

"You bastard," the punk hissed. "I'll teach you a lesson you won't ever forget. You hear me, jerk? I'm going to take you apart."

Jacob rolled sideways across the rear fender of the car and came up from a low, fierce crouch. He caught hold of the man's foot and yanked hard. As the attacker lost his balance, Jacob came down on top of him, aiming a slicing karate blow at the vulnerable point where the neck met the shoulder. The assailant crumpled and fell. The one in the trunk stirred and tried to rise.

Jacob gasped for air and glanced around for the knife. It had gotten kicked under the car. He didn't feel like crawling around on his hands and knees to get it, so he sprinted painfully across the concrete to grab the length of metal pipe that had been dropped earlier.

Just as his fist closed around it he heard the gate of the parking garage grate open. A pair of headlights speared the shadows. For an instant the tableau of violence was illuminated beneath the twin spotlights. Then the car pulled forward, effectively creating a barrier between Jacob and his assailants.

"Come on, Link, let's get out of here!" The man in the trunk staggered to his feet and grabbed his friend by the arm. "Move it, man, we got to get out of here!"

Jacob made a halfhearted effort to get around the newly arrived car, but he knew he wasn't going to make it. The two men, obviously strongly motivated in spite of their injuries, staggered to the still-open garage door and scrambled beneath it as it started to descend. By the time Jacob reached the wall switch that opened the door from the inside, the two had disappeared into the night.

Jacob swore, his body vibrating with the tension produced by the aftereffects of physical combat. He was vaguely aware of a warm, salty trickle down his chin and he absently wiped the blood off on his cuff. Then, realizing what he had just done, he glared in disgust at the ruined shirt. He had wanted to look his best this evening. He had wasted endless moments back in Portland choosing the right tie to go with this shirt and now both were a mess, thanks to those two punks.

"Dammit to hell," he muttered, swinging around to glower at the innocent driver of the car that had unwittingly provided getaway protection for the two jerks.

"What's going on here?" the man inside the car asked nervously as he eyed the blood and dirt on Jacob's clothing.

"Typical parking garage accident," Jacob explained.

8

EMILY DROVE into the parking garage feeling depressed in spite of the blue ribbon that was attached to the elegantly simple floral design sitting beside her. She knew exactly what was causing her depression. Some silly, optimistic part of her had actually expected Jacob to show up at the flower show.

She had been counting on it, she admitted to herself as she parked the car and got out. She had been pinning all her hopes on the expectation. She should have known better. A couple of dozen yellow roses and a note of apology had obviously not been enough to soothe his wounded ego.

Men, as she had just finished telling Diane over the victory drink her assistant had insisted on buying, were more trouble than they were worth.

She went around to the other side of the car and removed the flower arrangement that had brought her the ribbon that evening. Diane had been wrong, Emily told herself without much pleasure. The judges this year had been impressed by subtlety. She was glad she had followed her instincts and concentrated on a simple, graceful design of tiny orchids and curving vines. Using only minimal materials, she had made a final arrangement that had somehow evoked a quiet jungle pool. One judge had remarked that just looking at the design gave the viewer a feeling of elegant serenity.

Diane had been thrilled with the blue ribbon, Emily reminded herself as she walked to the elevators. Maybe tomorrow or the next day, she, too, would take some genuine pleasure in her accomplishment. Right now all she could think of was that Jacob had not forgiven her.

She rode up to her floor in an empty elevator and fumbled with her keys in the hall outside her door. She wondered what Jacob had done with the roses. Somehow, she had thought he would like them. In spite of his hardness there was a part of him that she knew responded to flowers. She had seen the way he handled them in the shop. He used the same tender touch that he used when he handled her. Perhaps she had only been fooling herself.

She opened the door and stepped into the apartment.

And stopped short, a tiny scream on her lips as she realized the living room light was on and the chair near the window was occupied.

"Don't panic," Jacob advised laconically as he got up. "It's not as bad as it looks."

"Jacob! What on earth are you doing here? What happened to you?" Emily set her flower arrangement down on a nearby table and stared at him. "You're bleeding."

"Still?" He frowned down at the damp cloth he held in one hand and then wiped his cut lip with it. "Damn. I thought that had stopped."

"There's blood all over your shirt. And your mouth. And you've got a bruise under your eye." Emily finally came unstuck from the floor and moved forward. "What happened to you?" She hurried toward him, alarm in her wide eyes and then she stopped directly in front of him, staring at his bruised face. "Did you have an accident?"

"You could say that." He smiled crookedly, wincing at the effort. His eyes gleamed. "No kiss for the wounded hero?"

"*Oh, Jacob.*" She threw her arms around him.

"Ouch!"

Instantly she released him. "Your ribs, too?"

"I'm not as young as I used to be," he confessed. He touched her parted lips with the callused tip of his thumb and his gaze softened. "I got the flowers, sweetheart."

"My flowers weren't responsible for this."

"True. A couple of punks waiting downstairs in your garage were responsible for this. About the flowers, honey. I want you to know how much—"

"You were attacked?" Emily yelped. "In my garage?"

"I've been telling you since the first time I saw it that your garage was potentially dangerous. You know, when the kid brought the roses to my door I thought there had been a mistake. I assumed they must have been meant for someone else and I—"

"I've never had any problem in that garage and neither has anyone else in the building," she interrupted forcefully, scanning him for more evidence of wounds. "Oh, once or twice a prowler got in and swiped a couple of tape decks, but that's all. There's never been anything like this in the whole time I've lived here. Jacob, this is awful. Did you call the police?"

"Yes. Emily—"

"Maybe we should call the building manager. Or have you already done it?" She looked up at him with worried eyes. "I wonder what those two punks could have wanted?"

"It was probably just another straightforward robbery attempt that went awry. Happens all the time in the city. Maybe they were going to use the garage elevators to gain access to the apartments upstairs," Jacob explained impatiently. "Listen, Emily, I want to tell you how much I—"

"How long ago did it happen? Have you seen a doctor?"

He groaned and abruptly reached out to fold his arms around her. He wrapped her close to him, heedless of his own soreness. One hand twisted gently in her hair so that he could bury her face against his hard chest.

The tactic effectively silenced her. When she was no longer in a position to hurl questions at him, Jacob bent his head and murmured into her hair, "Hush, Emily. Everything's under control. The police and the building manager left twenty minutes ago. No one's holding his breath hoping for an immediate arrest. This sort of thing happens all the time."

"Jacob . . ." Her voice was muffled against his shirt. Emily tried to pull free and discovered she was trapped. Jacob's arms around her were warm and tender but they were also as immovable as iron.

"Believe it or not, I've got more important things to talk about right now."

"Such as?"

His big hand moved in her hair and his other slid down her spine to the curve of her hip. He urged her lower body into the hard cradle of his thighs. "Such as two dozen yellow roses and a very short note of apology."

She managed to get her head up so that she could meet his eyes. "What's the matter?" she demanded waspishly. "Was the note too short?"

His gaze was fierce and warm. "No, the note was not too short. Emily, no one's ever sent me flowers before, let alone two dozen yellow roses."

She smiled tremulously. "You've probably never dated a florist before."

"I can't argue that. But that's not the point."

"What is the point, Jacob?"

He shook his head and framed her questioning face between his strong hands. "The point is, I should have been the one to send you the flowers and the note of apology."

Emily stared up at him. "What's that supposed to mean?"

"It means I was wrong to demand the apology from you in the first place. I shouldn't have jumped all over you for that scene in your father's study. You weren't using me to get back at your family. It's not in you to use someone else to get your revenge. I should have realized you were being honest when you told me you had threatened everyone with those damned shares just to protect me. You've always been honest with me, Emily."

Emily sighed with relief. She leaned her head back down on his shoulder. Her arms stole carefully around his waist. "When did you come to that conclusion?"

"About you being so honest?"

"No, about my having tried blackmail to protect you."

"Very early this morning," he admitted. "Amazing what two sleepless nights will do for a man's thinking ability. It finally dawned on me that you've got enough Ravenscroft blood in you to fight for something you want. You proved that when you went ahead and got the loan for your florist shop. But you're not enough of a Ravenscroft to use me or anyone else to plot revenge against your whole family. Not just for the sake of getting even with them for their meddling over the years. You really did think you were protecting me, didn't you?"

She nodded slowly. "I was so afraid they would find a means to drive you away from me. They don't like the idea of us having an affair."

Jacob appeared unconcerned by that. He smiled faintly and curled his hand around the nape of her neck. "The flowers arrived when I was in the middle of packing to drive up here so I could tell you I was sorry I had overreacted."

Emily's eyes widened. "You were going to do the apologizing?"

"Uh-huh." He bent his head to kiss her lightly on the brow. "But you beat me to it."

"Oh, Jacob, that's so sweet." Emily was enchanted. "You were actually going to apologize to me? I can't believe it." Without thinking, she hugged him tightly. Jacob sucked air painfully, and she instantly released him. "Oh, dear, I didn't mean to hurt you. Are you sure you're all right? Maybe we'd better get you to an emergency room."

"I'll live," he assured her. "I don't need a doctor."

"What happened to those two thugs who attacked you?" she demanded with a frown.

"They took off when another car drove into the garage. I gave the cops the descriptions, but, like I said, I'm not holding my breath." He scowled down at her. "I'd like to know why the idea of my apologizing is such a strange one for you to swallow."

She flushed and stepped back with a small, shaky laugh. "Ravenscrofts in general aren't big on apologies. They always figure they're in the right in the first place."

Jacob's eyes gleamed thoughtfully. "I'm not a Ravenscroft, remember?"

"I know, but you always seemed to be on the same side as the rest of my family," she reminded him bluntly. "You were always aligned with Dad and Drake and the rest of them. You were so much like them in so many ways. I guess I lumped you in with the others, and it always seemed to be me against the rest of you. And you were never big on apologizing, either, Jacob. Admit it. I put up with a lot from all of you over the years, and nobody ever said he was sorry. You weren't any better about it than the others. You all took the attitude that I was the one who should do the apologizing."

Jacob grinned wryly. "That's because we all thought you should appreciate the fact that we were only acting in your best interests."

"Hah."

"I guess it must have been hard at times, hmm? All those people, me included, trying to tell you how to live your life?" Jacob reached out and pulled her back into his arms.

"Very hard." She touched him gently, conscious of his bruises, and inhaled the exciting, male scent of his body.

"Emily," he said in a new and more urgent tone, "I'll admit that your family and I are probably guilty of overprotecting you on occasion, but the truth is there were plenty of times when you needed that protection. Look at how far Morrell got with you before you found out he was just using you."

"I wish everyone would stop throwing Damon in my face." Emily tugged free of Jacob's grasp. "I was only dating the man. We weren't having an affair and we certainly were not planning marriage, as my parents feared. He did not get very far with me at all."

"Maybe you weren't planning either an affair or marriage, but Morrell was."

"For Pete's sake, that doesn't mean I would have meekly gone along with him," Emily snapped. Her mood was beginning to shift from blissful relief at finding Jacob in her apartment to a familiar sense of defensiveness. "I decided two years ago I would never marry."

Jacob's eyes were suddenly alive with an unidentifiable emotion. "You did?" he asked softly.

Emily tried to treat the whole thing casually. "I took your advice. I came to the conclusion you were right. Marriage was an institution for fools. I believe those were your exact words. And in my case, I had the additional worry of trying to find a man who wouldn't want control of RI. All in all, I decided the sensible thing to do was never to marry. So you see, there was never any real danger of Damon talking me into marrying him. Can't anyone give me a little credit for being able to take care of myself?"

"Honey, I'm sorry. Again. The last thing I want to do tonight is lecture you or chew you out or annoy you." He came up behind her and wrapped his arms around her. Then he bent his head and nuzzled the warm, sweetly scented place behind her left ear. "Let's forget Morrell and your family and those two punks in the garage. We've got better things to do."

Emily sighed and let herself sink back into his warmth. "It's very hard for me to stay annoyed with you, Jacob."

"Good." He kissed the curve of her shoulder with satisfaction. "What was that you were carrying when you came through the door a few minutes ago?"

"My floral design. I won, Jacob. I won first place in the professional show category." For the first time that evening, she could enjoy the victory.

He turned her around in his arms, grinning down at her. "Congratulations. I can't say I'm surprised." He walked over to where the winning arrangement sat on a table. Jacob studied it for a long moment, moving around it to see it from all angles.

Emily realized she was holding her breath. When he turned back to her he was smiling with an odd satisfaction.

"It's perfect," he said, coming back toward her. "Exotic and tempting and a little mystifying. Just like you." His fingers went to the buttons of her blouse. "We have a lot to celebrate tonight. And I can't think of any better way to do it than to take you to bed. I was a fool to leave you alone at that hotel in Portland. But at least I learn from my mistakes." His eyes were cloudy with desire.

"What about your bruises?" Emily asked anxiously. She was vividly aware of the exciting roughness of his fingertips as he undid the buttons of her blouse. "I wouldn't want to hurt you."

"Just be gentle with me, okay?" he said with a rare, wicked grin.

She responded to his teasing with impulsive delight. Something about Jacob always seemed to release the sensual, daring side of her nature. No other man had ever had that effect on her. Emily reached up and put her arms around his neck, urging his head down to hers.

"All you'll have to do is lie back and enjoy it," she promised in a reckless, throaty whisper.

"Is that right?"

"Trust me." She brushed her mouth lightly against his, careful not to hurt his cut lip. He groaned and his fingers fumbled slightly as he finished undoing her buttons. All of a sudden Emily was brimming with excitement and the thrill of feminine power.

Deliberately she loosened his tie, letting the two ends dangle around his neck while she went to work on his shirt. She paused briefly when she saw the bloodstain on the cuff, but when she looked up at Jacob she knew he did not want to waste any time explaining it. His eyes were glittering now with a familiar hunger. She dropped the shirt on the floor, leaving the striped tie still dangling down his broad chest.

"My turn," Jacob muttered, starting to peel off her blouse.

"No, not yet." She caught his prowling fingers in both hands and held them still. She smiled up at him with a sensual promise. "You're wounded and out of action tonight. I'm in charge." She unbuckled his belt and found his zipper.

"Did you learn this in your assertiveness training class?" he asked with deep interest as he stepped obediently out of his slacks.

She looked down at the hard, thrusting shape of his manhood outlined by his white briefs. The knowledge that he wanted her, that his body was vibrating with his desire, inspired her. Her fingers trailed over his shoulders. "My instructor insisted we all learn to improvise so that we would be able to handle any occasion that arose."

"Something is arising, all right." Jacob captured her questing fingers and guided them down below his waist. He held her hand against him, letting her feel his readiness. "Think you can handle it?"

She touched him intimately, cupping him gently. The heat of him filled her palm, and she shivered as her own desire flared. She drew a deep breath and then wriggled her fingers free of his insistent hand. "I graduated at the top of my assertiveness training course," she assured him. She took hold of the dangling ends of his tie and boldly began to lead him down the hall to her bedroom.

For the first time Jacob balked. "Uh, Emily, this bit with the tie may be overdoing things a little. I feel like a bull being led out of his stall." He chuckled slightly and started to pull the tie out of her grasp.

Emily tightened her hold on the silk strips. "Think of yourself as the spoils of battle."

His eyes narrowed slightly. "Little witch" was all he said, but his hand fell away and he allowed himself to be led into the bedroom.

Emily was delighted with the small triumph. It was the second one this evening. "First a blue ribbon and now a taste of real power," she said with a soft laugh. "What an evening."

"Just so long as you don't try to pin that ribbon on me," he growled.

"Don't worry. I've got more interesting things to do to you than pin ribbons on you." She led him into the white-on-white bedroom and pushed him lightly onto the bed. He went down obediently under her hands. She stood looking at him, trying to think of what to do next.

He sensed her uncertainty and grinned invitingly. "Tell me about these interesting things you're planning to do to me."

The teasing element in his voice was enough to goad her into further action. Emily gave him an up-from-under look through her lashes and then, feeling more daring than ever, began to undress herself. The gray fire that leaped into his eyes was ample indication that she was on the right track.

Jacob said nothing as first her blouse and then her skirt slipped to the floor, but his eyes roved over her with unmistakable possessiveness. When she began to slip off her bra and panties, there was nothing humorous left in his expression. He was aroused and hungry for her.

"Come here, witch," he ordered softly when she stood nude before him. He did not move from where he lay back against her pillows but he held out his hand in a not-so-subtle command.

Emily ignored the extended palm. She smiled at him, instead, confident now of her power over him. It was so good to know that she had the same effect on him as he had on her. Paying no attention to his imperiously out-stretched fingers, she moved closer to the side of the bed.

"There's no rush," she said, aware of the fire in her own pulse. He looked so big and powerful and sexy lying there sprawled across her bed. She could hardly believe he was hers.

"No rush? Lady, I'm burning. If you don't come here and make love to me right now, I'm liable to find out firsthand what's meant by spontaneous combustion."

Emily felt herself turning hot and languorous under his intent gaze. Her knees were getting weak. If she did not climb onto that bed with him, and soon, she would probably collapse.

"I wouldn't want you to go up in flames. Not just yet," she assured him as she moved down beside him on the bed. She could feel the sexual tension in him from one end of the bed to the other. Her fingers made small circles around the flat, masculine nipples. Then she allowed one of her legs to tangle with his.

He shuddered heavily and looked up at her with a combination of frustration and demand in his eyes. "Are you by any chance turning into a tease?"

"What if I am?" She picked up one end of his tie and trailed it through the hair on his chest.

"Then I'm a doomed man. I'll never survive being teased by you tonight. My physical condition is just not strong enough. I'm weak and wounded and at your mercy. Have pity."

"Well, since you put it that way, I suppose I can be generous."

Jacob's mouth curved with satisfaction. "Somehow I thought you might be." He drew a hand down her back, exploring the gentle contours there before moving his palm lower. He tightened his fingers around her hip.

It was Emily's turn to shudder. She nestled closer to him and began dropping light, soft kisses down the length of his body. Jacob twisted his hands in her hair and watched her through passion-slitted eyes.

"That feels so good," he growled. "Honey, you don't know what you do to me. So good."

All thought of teasing him fled. Emily was beyond playing sexy games now. She was thrilled with his response and trembling with the force of her own. Her kisses became deeper and more intimate. She explored the inside of his thigh with soft fingers until he was rumbling far back in his throat.

"Are you purring?" she asked, lifting her head briefly to meet his eyes.

"Not yet. But I think I will be soon." He reached down to grasp her shoulders and ease her down on top of him. "Make me purr, sweet witch."

She smiled dreamily and fitted herself carefully to him. He was large and hard and he filled her with a slow, aching thoroughness. Emily sank down onto him, mindful of his sore ribs, anxious to give him what he wanted without hurting him in the process.

"Gentle as a flower," he whispered with aching longing as he lifted his hips and drove himself more deeply into her.

Emily gave herself up to the sweeping passion, loving him as gently and completely as she could, glorying in the tenderness and the underlying power that was so much a part of him. Together they raced for the heights and threw themselves over the edge, only to be caught and cushioned by the warm, sensual currents of release.

And when at last it was over, Jacob did, indeed, purr.

EMILY WAS THE ONE who felt like purring the next morning when she awoke in Jacob's arms. The room was full of rare Seattle sunlight, and the man lying beside her was hers. She hugged the knowledge to herself with glee. She was having an affair with Jacob Stone and she was happy. She had no way of knowing how long her good fortune would last, but she had decided not to look too far into the future. She would grab what happiness she could with both hands and enjoy it now. She propped herself up on one elbow and gazed down at her man.

Jacob stirred and yawned, his arm tightening around Emily. He opened his eyes and saw her smiling down at him. A slow grin etched the hard line of his mouth. "What are you looking at, sexy?"

"You."

"Like what you see?"

She toyed with the crisp hair on his chest. "It'll do until something better comes along," she retorted flippantly.

"Is that right?" he asked with unexpected roughness, turning over on his side to pin her beneath him. "Are you expecting something better to come along soon?"

Emily blinked, realizing he had not taken the joke well. "I was just teasing, Jacob."

"I know." He threw one leg over hers. "But some subjects are off-limits when it comes to early-morning jokes. Replacing me is one of them."

She arched her eyebrows. "I'll remember that."

"You do that." He kissed the hollow of her throat, his hand closing over one of her breasts.

She realized he was not teasing her in return. There was a hard current under his words. Emily slid her fingers deep into his tousled hair. For the first time she wondered if he might be feeling insecure in their relationship. It was hard to imagine Jacob Stone feeling insecure about anything. "Jacob?"

"Hmm?" He was kissing the valley between her breasts.

"Were you really going to apologize first to me yesterday?"

"Yeah. I was going to get on my hands and knees." He dipped his tongue into the small hollow of her stomach and smiled to himself when she trembled delicately. "But you beat me to it. I'm going to make it up to you, though. You deserve a proper apology and I'm going to see that you get it."

"Interesting. How do you plan to do that?"

He raised his head and looked down at her intently. "I'm going to take you away for a few days. We'll go to the coast. Rent a cabin. Just you and me."

Emily's eyes widened in surprise. "What about my shop? Jacob, I haven't planned any vacations in the near future. I don't know if I can get away on a moment's notice. You know how it is when you run your own business."

"Diane can handle things for a few days, can't she? We'll call her this morning and tell her she's going to be on her own for a while. She won't mind. You must have left her in charge before."

"Well, yes, it's just that I hadn't planned—" Emily broke off, frowning slightly.

Jacob brushed her mouth with his own. "I want you all to myself for a while, honey. We need some time alone together. Time to talk. Time to plan."

Emily searched his eyes. "Time to plan?"

"There are things we need to discuss," he said gently. "We can't continue much longer with me down in Portland and you up here. It'll drive me nuts not being able to live with you. I want you with me on a regular basis. Come with me to the coast where we can be alone to talk it all out."

Emily caught her breath. "You're moving very quickly," she whispered.

"I've waited a long time for you. I don't intend to waste any more time." His warm, hard palm slipped down over her stomach and into the soft hair that concealed her feminine secrets. He claimed the hidden territory, finding the moist warmth that was already gathering there. "Let me take you away for a few days, sweetheart."

Emily stirred languidly beneath his touch, her body responding to him with an immediacy that still took her by surprise. He wanted to be alone with her to discuss their future. She was terrified of any such discussion. A few minutes ago she had been giving herself a stern lecture on the subject of living for the present and not even thinking about what lay ahead.

But a trip to the coast with her lover sounded wonderful. And if he wanted to discuss their future, perhaps she would let him. After all, she was entitled to a few daydreams. Happiness blossomed within her. She tightened her arms around his neck.

"All right. Yes. Yes, please, Jacob. I would like that very much."

"We'll leave this morning as soon as you arrange things with Diane." He bent down to kiss away any protest she might still feel inclined to make.

But Emily wasn't putting up any more resistance to the idea of going away with Jacob for a few days. In fact, she wasn't putting up any resistance at all. Instead she was gathering him to her, wrapping her legs around him as he moved to sheath himself deeply within her welcoming warmth. After that there was no more thought of resistance at all.

AN HOUR LATER Emily stepped into the shower, aware of a few sensual aches in regions of her body that were not yet accustomed to Jacob's passionate lovemaking. She turned her face up to the hot water and closed her eyes for a long, blissful moment.

She was going away for a few days with Jacob. It seemed to Emily that the world was a very good place that morning. She tried to concentrate on what to pack for the short vacation at the beach and as her mind turned to more prosaic matters she remembered she needed a new blade in her razor. It wouldn't do to leave on a passionate vacation with her lover without first shaving her legs. She left the water running as she quickly stepped out of the shower and went to open a drawer near the sink.

She was standing there, dripping, trying to find the new blades without benefit of her glasses when she caught the soft, muffled sound of a man's voice.

Emily turned her head toward the door, wondering if Jacob was talking to someone on the phone. Perhaps Diane had called. It would ruin everything if Diane was phoning in sick.

Emily opened the door and leaned out into the hall to call a question to Jacob. He was talking in a low, intent voice, but she caught a few of the words and they froze her in her wet tracks. Jacob was not talking to Diane. He was talking to her brother.

"No, I can't prove a damned thing, Drake. But I don't believe in coincidences. It's not as if people get attacked in Emily's garage on a regular basis. It might have been a piece of bad luck. God knows I've been in the wrong place at the wrong time on previous occasions. But this time I'm a little suspicious. I'm not going to let Emily take any chances. She's too vulnerable and Morrell knows it." He paused, listening. "No, you won't be able to reach us. I don't know yet where we'll be staying. Don't worry about it. I'll contact you. I'll keep her out of the way for a few days while you and Giff make your move."

Emily was vaguely aware that she was creating a large, damp spot on her white carpet. She was also cold. But she could not seem to find the strength to move back into the steamy warmth of the bathroom. She listened to the remainder of the call with fatalistic attention.

"How the hell should I know what approach you should take? I don't work for you anymore, remember? My only interest in all this is keeping Emily out of the way. You want some free advice? Try digging around the Satterly deal. There was something off base about that right from the start. We knew that. Check with Satterly's administrative assistant. He's the kind who will talk for a price. I've used him before. If you look hard enough, you should be able to find something you can use."

Emily finally recovered control over her muscles. She walked slowly into her bedroom, the shower still running behind her, and reached for a terry-cloth robe. She belted it in place and went down the hall to the living room where Jacob was just completing his phone call.

He was standing with his back to her, gazing out the window as he spoke. He sounded impatient and determined. Emily came to a halt in the doorway and stood looking at his bare, broad shoulders. Jacob was barefoot, wearing only a pair of jeans. He had not finished dressing after he'd gotten out of the shower a few minutes ago. He'd obviously waited until he'd heard the shower running again and then he'd reached for the phone.

"Yeah, I'll give you a call in a couple of days to see how things are going. Don't worry about Emily. I'll take care of her." Jacob tossed the phone back down into its cradle and caught sight of Emily standing very still in the doorway. He swore softly. "I thought you were in the shower."

"That's obvious. If you hadn't thought that, you wouldn't have made that call to my brother."

"Emily, I didn't want to worry you." He watched her assessingly.

"So thoughtful." She tightened the sash of the robe and moved a couple of steps into the room before stopping again. "Always looking out for my best interests. Such a loyal RI man. Always willing to sacrifice himself to keep the Ravenscrofts' wayward daughter out of trouble."

Jacob ran a hand through his hair in a disgusted manner. "I guess you're going to read all the wrong things into that phone call, aren't you? I had a feeling you would. That's why I didn't want you to hear it."

Her eyes widened with mock innocence. "How should I interpret that phone call, Jacob? Suppose you tell me exactly what's going on. What was the real reason you wanted to take me to the coast for a few days?"

He regarded her consideringly. Emily had seen that look before, and she did not like it. He was wondering exactly how much to tell her. It made her aware once more of just how Jacob and her family had always dealt with her.

"Emily..."

Suddenly she'd had enough. "Forget it. I don't want to hear any more. I'm sure you were only acting in my *best interests*." She swung around and started back down the hall to her waiting shower. She would be lucky if there was any hot water left.

"Emily, wait just one damned minute. As long as you overheard me talking to your brother, you might as well hear it all."

Jacob came after her, reaching her just as she stepped into the steamy bathroom. His hand closed around her shoulder, tugging her around to face him. Unable to escape his hold, she looked up at him with stormy eyes.

"I'd appreciate it if you would let go of me. I'm going to be late for work as it is."

"You're not going in to work today. You're coming to the coast with me."

"Why? Because you've arrived at some wild conclusion about those two punks who attacked you in the garage? You think Damon might have sent them? That's ridiculous. I don't need any protection from Damon."

Temper flared in Jacob's grim eyes. "Is that right? What about the time he assaulted you right here in your own apartment?"

"That was hardly a full-scale assault. He just tried to kiss me, that's all. He was upset. I could have handled him."

"The hell you could. He would have raped you if I hadn't arrived when I did. He was out for vengeance and you were the most convenient target."

"He would not have raped me. He was angry but he wouldn't have hurt me."

"That's what you think. All he cares about is hurting a Ravenscroft. He was going to use you to cripple the firm, and when that failed he intended to take out his frustration on you."

"Even if that much is true, why would he send those punks after you?"

Jacob sucked in his breath and his hands closed more tightly around her shoulders. "How do you know they were after me? Maybe they were waiting for you last night, Emily. Maybe Morrell sent them to grab you. Maybe they tried to take me out because they saw me as being in the way. We can't take any risks, Emily."

Emily shuddered as the realization hit home. It wasn't just herself and her wounded feelings she had to consider right now. She had to think about the possibility of Jacob being in danger. "So this is the real reason you're so eager for us to take a little trip to the coast. As usual, you're just acting for the family, protecting me. I would have appreciated some honesty, Jacob. I get very tired of being sheltered and protected. In fact, I'm damned sick of it."

He closed his eyes briefly and growled a low curse. "I'm sorry, Emily. I guess the habit of sheltering you is too strong. Hell, it isn't just a habit. It's my gut instinct. I just want to keep you safe, sweetheart."

"Tell me something," Emily asked wearily. "Were we scheduled to ever get around to discussing our future while we sat out there in that cozy cabin on the coast? Or was that just a lure to coax me into going with you?"

"We were going to discuss the future, all right," he muttered. "I was planning on asking you to marry me."

9

"MARRY YOU? You're serious?" Emily sat strapped into the passenger seat of Jacob's Mercedes, feeling bemused and totally disconcerted. She had been feeling that way since Jacob had made his unexpected announcement in the bathroom. Her stunned reaction had given him the advantage. Before she'd quite realized what was happening, she had found herself packed up and stashed in his car. Jacob had even handled the call to Diane, instructing her to take over at the shop until further notice.

Emily was beginning to realize why her father had relied on Jacob for so many odd jobs during the past few years. He was definitely the take-charge type.

"Of course I'm serious," Jacob said, easing the car through morning traffic. "What makes you think I'm not?"

She hedged. "Well, for one thing, you told me two years ago you'd probably never marry again."

"Emily, that was then and this is now. Two years ago I was ending a bad marriage and convinced I'd probably never be able to have you. I was angry at life in general, and I probably said a lot of things that I would now prefer to forget."

Emily shifted uneasily in the seat. "But why marriage, Jacob? We can be together, if that's what you want, the way we have been for the past few days."

"No," he stated bluntly, "we can't. You might be able to survive the strain but I won't."

"If you're talking about the situation with Damon Morrell and your suspicions about him, I don't think that constitutes a solid reason for something as drastic as marriage." Emily was feeling goaded. "I appreciate your loyalty to the family, naturally, but I think marrying me to protect me from Damon is going a little too far above and beyond the call of duty. I also doubt that in this case my family would appreciate your sacrifice. But the main point is that I don't need the protection. I have said it a thousand times in the past and I will say it again—*I can take care of myself.*"

"Don't be ridiculous, Emily. You know damned good and well I'm not marrying you in order to protect you from Morrell. There are easier ways of handling him, believe me."

"Then why do you want to marry me?" she exploded.

"For the usual reasons," he shot back.

"Such as?"

He slanted her a narrow look and made an obvious bid for his patience. "Such as the fact that we are very strongly attracted to each other, although I'll admit a casual onlooker might not think so if he saw us bickering like this. What a mess. I never intended for it to be like this. I'd planned on a cozy fire, a nice glass of wine, maybe a few flowers. I was even going to wear a tie. I wanted it to be right."

Emily listened to him, her pulse pounding with awareness. "Attracted to each other." Surely that wasn't the extent of his feelings for her. She knew him well enough to know he would never marry her just to satisfy a physical attraction. Besides, it wasn't necessary to marry her for such a reason. She was more than willing to give herself to him out of marriage.

Her voice was a little unsteady as she said coolly, "If you wanted it to be right, you shouldn't have tried to kill two birds with one stone. Taking me away to the coast so that I'd be conveniently out of Damon's reach does not go well with the promise of a romantic interlude. I never did like my family's habit of mixing business with pleasure."

"*Business with pleasure?*" Jacob's grip on the wheel was savage. "Is that how you see it?"

"That's how it looks to me," she retorted.

"I don't believe this. I refuse to believe it. You're being deliberately obstinate and you know it. You and your damned assertiveness training. Why don't you just keep quiet for a while until you've had a chance to cool down and think things over?"

"Now you're telling me to shut up?" she asked with grave interest. "While you make sweeping decisions about my future? That has a familiar ring to it."

"Emily, I'm basically very tolerant when it comes to dealing with you. I don't think you have any idea of just how tolerant I am about your crazy ways. But right now you're coming very close to the line. I suggest we keep quiet for a while. Maybe we both need to cool down. Let me know when you feel like having an intelligent, reasonable discussion on the subject of marriage."

"I'll do that," she agreed far too sweetly. He could wait until hell froze over. She folded her arms and sat back in her seat, glaring out the window. She was determined not to break the silence he had imposed. She had apologized once to this man, even though she had done nothing that warranted it. She was not about to give in again. It was up to him to reopen the argument.

But it was a long drive to the coast, and Jacob seemed contented to concentrate on the road ahead. Emily was not nearly so sanguine. She was feeling put-upon and abused, and she was spoiling for a fight. Unfortunately she had been around Jacob long enough to know that her odds of winning were limited. One did not wage open warfare easily with a man like Jacob Stone. He was far too accustomed to winning.

Assertiveness did not always mean a confrontation, she reminded herself. Sometimes it meant biding one's time. She had plenty to think about before she made her decision.

Marriage.

Jacob's proposal staggered her. It would have been just as disconcerting even if it had been delivered under more romantic circumstances. Marriage was the one thing she had pushed to the back of her mind whenever she thought about her relationship with Jacob.

The raw fact was that she was still trying to work out a way to convince her family to tolerate her affair with Jacob. Marriage was simply out of the question.

Matters were moving much too fast, Emily thought. It was going to be difficult enough to conduct an affair. Until now she hadn't allowed herself to look very far into the future of her relationship with Jacob. She could only think of it on a day-to-day basis. Emily did not want to even contemplate how rough things might get if she told her family she was going to marry Jacob.

By the time they reached the coast and found accommodations in one of the cabins of a beachfront lodge, Emily was sick of being silent. She was also more confused and anxious than ever. It was clear someone was going to have to take the initiative.

Feeling more put-upon than ever, she opened the car door, got out and reached for her bag. "Nice spot," she muttered, scanning the windswept beach. There was a storm moving in from the ocean. It would hit land soon.

"Glad you like it," Jacob said laconically as he carried the luggage inside the small cabin.

Emily sighed and followed him inside. The cabin was surprisingly comfortable. There was a large fireplace built into one wall, a tiny kitchen and a sitting area near the window. The big bed occupied center stage in the room.

Jacob set the luggage down and turned to her. "Put on your jacket and we'll go for a walk on the beach. I could use the exercise after that drive."

"Please."

He cocked a brow at her. "Please what?"

"You're supposed to say please put on your jacket and then you're supposed to ask me if I would like a walk on the beach. You're not supposed to issue orders about it."

"I get it. Not romantic, hmm?" But the hard line of his mouth had softened and his eyes were speculative.

"It's not a question of romance. It's a question of good manners."

"Someday I'd like to get my hands on whoever taught that class in assertiveness training you took. Okay, would you like to go for a walk on the beach?"

"That sounds nice."

"Then would you please put on your jacket?"

"Sure," Emily said, giving him a saucy glare. She shrugged into her lined yellow windbreaker. "Ready when you are."

"Such an accommodating woman." Jacob pulled on his slate-gray jacket and opened the door. "After you," he said with exaggerated politeness.

Head high, Emily walked back out into the gray afternoon. Neither of them said a word until they had reached the water's edge and turned to walk along the packed sand. They paced side by side but they kept their hands stubbornly thrust into the pockets of their jackets. It was Jacob who spoke first.

"All right," he said, "tell me why you don't want to marry me."

"I never said I didn't want to marry you," Emily hedged.

He ignored that. "Is it because I'm not an especially impressive specimen at the moment? I know that if you look at me objectively, you could find some faults."

"For instance?" Emily challenged.

He shrugged. "I'm not currently employed, for one thing."

"True. But I could give you a job delivering flowers."

Jacob smiled briefly. "You'd like being in a position to give me orders, wouldn't you?"

"It's a tantalizing thought. Go on. What other faults do you have?"

"You're really getting into this, aren't you? Well, let's see, I was involved in a very unpleasant divorce."

"Not your fault," she told him magnanimously. "I remember Leanna. Nothing you did would have made her happy. Continue."

"I don't share your social background." He looked out to sea.

"I don't share it, either," Emily said with a grimace. "My social background, such as it is, is largely a product of my parents' imagination and wishful thinking."

Jacob nodded, accepting that. "There's something else."

"What?"

"For a long time you've viewed me as the enemy. I was always on your family's side. It always seemed to be a case of you against us."

"I'll grant you that point," she agreed with alacrity.

Jacob came to an abrupt halt and reached out to stop her. His hand clamped around her arm. "Is that the main problem, Emily? You still see me as the enemy?"

"I've never seen you as the enemy," she told him softly.

"But I was always the bad guy. What was it you called me? The family's enforcer?"

"Sometimes it seemed that way," she admitted.

"Is that why you're trying to wriggle out of marrying me? Because of the role I played for RI?"

"No." But she was beginning to get agitated. He was homing in on the truth. "Jacob, please, there's no point in this. Why don't we just enjoy what we have together for as long as we can?"

"You owe me an explanation. Apparently I'm good enough to sleep with but not good enough to marry you."

"That's not true!"

"Then why won't you marry me?" he said through gritted teeth. His eyes were cold gray, bottomless pools. Then his eyes narrowed as he promptly jumped to a conclusion. "Dammit, Emily, you don't think I'm after those RI shares, do you?"

"No!" She threw up her hands in genuine shock. "Of course not. I've never once thought you might be after a chunk of RI."

Jacob's response was a wry smile. "Sometimes you are so sweet and trusting it scares the hell out of me. It's a possibility, you know."

"That you're scheming to marry me for my shares? No, it's not. You'd never interfere with RI," she declared staunchly. "Even if you did, you'd never use me to do it."

"Thank you for that much, at least. So what's the real reason?"

She gave up trying to evade the question. He wanted an answer. She might as well spell it out for him. "Jacob, don't you see that the marriage wouldn't have a chance? It wouldn't last. We'll be lucky to get away with having an affair for a few weeks or months," she whispered miserably. "It's all we can hope for."

"Why, dammit? I'll make you a good husband. I'll be faithful. I'll take care of you. The unemployed status is temporary and you know it. I'm not marrying you for your family connections."

"It's got nothing to do with any of that," she cried. "Please, Jacob . . ."

"Why won't you marry me?"

"Because my family would find a way to destroy the marriage and I couldn't bear it!" Emily yelled as the sea wind whipped her hair. Tears burned in her eyes. "Now do you understand? I just couldn't bear to watch them drive you away from me."

Jacob stared at her in astonishment. "That's the reason? You're afraid your family will object?"

"I'm not afraid of their objecting to the marriage, I'm afraid of them doing something about it." Emily wiped the back of her hand across her eyes and cursed the dampness. "I've tried to tell you. They've always been able to do something about situations they don't like. You should know. You've been the means they've used to fix those situations often enough. If we got married, they would find a way to convince you to leave me. I know they would."

Jacob's astonishment was slowly metamorphosing into another expression altogether. His eyes were full of gray fire now and his face was set in rigid lines. He was coldly furious. "That's the real reason you won't marry me? You've still got it fixed in your head that your family will find a way to get rid of me?"

Emily nodded in mute despair. "I know they would. They like you as an employee, Jacob. You've been very useful to them. But they don't want you as a son-in-law. And you wouldn't let me use the one defense I had against them. You refused to let me threaten them with the shares. There's nothing else that will stop them from interfering in our lives. You know that better than most people do. You should know what they're capable of doing."

"I wonder if you have any idea of what I'm capable of doing to you at the moment," Jacob asked harshly.

She blinked through her tears. His tone made her uneasy. "Jacob?"

He stood looking down at her, his gaze shadowed and cold. "What it really comes down to is that you don't trust me."

"That's not true." She was shocked at his interpretation.

"It's true, all right. You don't trust me to be able to deal with a bunch of Ravenscrofts. You don't think I can protect both myself and you from them."

She realized just how offended he really was and she was instantly contrite. "Oh, Jacob, I never meant to imply you couldn't take care of yourself, but you know what they're like. They've intimidated union leaders, corporate presidents and even a few politicians. They've handled everything from kidnapping to industrial espionage and come out on top. Furthermore, they've run off every serious boyfriend I've ever had."

"And deep down you're scared to death of them."

"I know how powerful they can be," she insisted. "I know how they can interfere in my life. They've done it often enough in the past. I don't want to run any more risks with our relationship than are absolutely necessary. I only had one bargaining tool and that was my stake in Ravenscroft International. The one time I tried to use that option to protect us, you were furious. When they find out I'm not really going to use the shares to keep them in line after all we'll be on borrowed time. Sooner or later everything will come crashing down around our ears." Her eyes brightened hopefully. "Maybe if you changed your mind and let me really use the threat . . ."

Jacob shook his head, disgusted as well as angry. "Forget it. I'm not going to let you threaten your family on my behalf. You're out of the blackmail business. It's not exactly a suitable sideline for a professional florist. I've come to a conclusion about those damned shares."

"What conclusion?"

"I suggest you sell them back to your family. Take the money and use it to open your second florist shop."

Emily's eyes widened. "I can't do that."

"Why not? You're not getting any income from them this way, and you don't like being tied to RI. Why are you hanging on to those shares?"

"I made a promise to Grandmother. Someday I'll tell you about it."

"All right, forget the shares, then. I don't care what you do with them so long as you don't use them as blackmail ammunition. That brings us back to us." Jacob started striding down the beach again, using his grip on Emily's arm to pull her along behind him. "Now let's deal with the main issue here. I assume we now have all the facts on the table? Your only reason for not accepting my proposal is that you think I'm such a wimp I can't stand up to your family?"

"That's not quite the way I would put it, Jacob," she retorted.

"I don't care how you phrase it, that's the bottom line, right?"

"Jacob, I'm trying to be reasonable."

"You're running scared," he corrected in a scathing tone. "You know, Emily, that's the one thing I wouldn't have expected from you. You've always at least tried to fight back."

"You know how much good it's done me in the past," she retorted. "I almost always lost and you know it. Sometimes you had a hand in my losing."

He winced. "The point is, you always tried. And you didn't always lose. You've been in business as a florist now for nearly two years, right? And you've told me yourself that your family has objected all along the way."

"That was different. I really wanted that shop. I wanted to run my own business and I loved flowers—" She broke off, biting her lip as she realized where that line of logic was leading.

"Exactly," Jacob said quietly as he watched her face. "You really wanted that shop and you loved working with flowers. When it came to getting what you really wanted and doing what you loved, you held your ground and your family hasn't been able to do a damned thing about it. Do you really want me, Emily? Do you want me as much as you wanted your own business?"

"Jacob," she whispered on a choked sob. She turned and crowded against him, burying her face against his shoulder. "I want you more than anything else in the world. But I'm so afraid of losing you."

His arms closed fiercely around her. "You say you want me more than anything else in the world. Then want me enough to take the risk of marrying me. Trust me, sweetheart."

Emily surrendered. There was no way out of the trap. She knew Jacob wasn't going to settle for anything less than marriage. She hugged him fiercely. "All right, Jacob." Somehow it was a tremendous relief to stop fighting him. Probably because deep inside she longed to believe that the marriage stood a chance.

"I think," Jacob said musingly as he pinned her close against him, "that we're going to make a slight detour from our original itinerary."

"A change of plans?" Emily looked up at him, her eyes still bright with tears. "Where are we going now?"

"Reno. We'll spend the night here and catch a plane to Nevada in the morning. It's my turn to limit my risks and I'm not taking any chances that you'll talk yourself out of this marriage."

EMILY WAS STILL IN SHOCK the next day when the jet set down in Reno. She stayed in shock all through the short, assembly line wedding service and didn't show any signs of coming out of it when Jacob checked into the huge, plush casino hotel.

He kept a close eye on her at dinner that night. Her appetite seemed off. Emily normally enjoyed her food, but tonight she just played with it. She was tense, jittery and uncertain.

This was not a normal case of bridal jitters. Jacob finally realized she was scared to death. She wasn't thinking of her wedding night or their future. She was dreading having to tell her family that she was married. Part of him was furious, but another part of him acknowledged that she thought she had some genuine basis for her fears. After all, one way or another, her family had managed to destroy the few serious relationships she'd had. On two occasions, Jacob himself had helped bring them to an end. Small wonder she was nervous about the outcome of her marriage.

But the measure of understanding he was able to summon up for her did not do much to cut through Jacob's annoyance. He wanted Emily to believe in him. By forcing her into marriage he had intended to more or less force her to demonstrate some faith in him.

There were a lot of things you could accomplish by force, Jacob knew. But it was beginning to look as if making a wife trust her husband's strength was not one of them.

He tried to take her mind off the subject by encouraging her to do some gambling. She promptly lost fifty dollars at the blackjack table. When he bought her several rolls of coins for the garish slot machines, she managed to lose every single quarter. He took her to see the lavish floor show and she did not smile once.

Some wedding night, Jacob decided. Maybe he had been wrong to rush her into this. But he had been terrified she would change her mind about accepting his proposal if he did not seize the moment. The frustration, he realized, had driven him to the edge of his temper.

"It's not normal, you know," Jacob told Emily forcefully that night as they walked into the extravagantly decorated hotel room. All the decor in the hotel had obviously been designed to make the visitor think he had wandered into a fantasy land. Unfortunately, Jacob thought, Emily seemed immune. She was still dwelling within her own grim reality.

"What's not normal?" Emily frowned questioningly as he closed and locked the door behind them.

"Your fear of your family. They're not exactly a pack of cutthroat thieves and murderers. You've blown them up in your mind until they're out of all proportion."

She sighed and sank onto the bed, the skirts of her new red-and-gold dinner dress swirling out around her. She had bought the dress earlier in one of the well-stocked boutiques downstairs. It had not done much for her mood, Jacob had noticed, even though she looked very sexy and dramatic in it. She was peering at him now through her glasses, her eyes thoughtful.

"You're probably right," she agreed. "Force of habit. I used to think of you that way, too. Large, powerful, intimidating. You know what? You haven't changed."

Jacob walked to the bed and stood in front of her. "Emily," he said gently, "Something has changed. You're my wife and I'm on your side." He bent down and pulled her to her feet. "The truth is, I've always been on your side. I love you, sweetheart. I've loved you since the day I carried you out of that damned cabin where that lunatic was holding you prisoner. It tore my guts out then to think that I could probably never have you. Every time your father or mother mentioned a new boyfriend in your life, I sweated. You'll never know what it did to me to learn you were planning to marry Carlton. And when I came back this last time and found you mixed up with Morrell, I wanted to go for his throat."

She was staring at him. "You love me?"

Jacob glowered at her. "Of course I love you. Do you think I'd go through all this if I didn't love you? What's the matter with you, woman? You never used to be dumb."

"Jacob, you've never said it. All you ever said was that you wanted me. I knew you had to be feeling something more than that or you wouldn't have wanted to marry me, but you've never actually said you loved me."

He really was going to lose his temper, Jacob decided. The only thing that was restraining him was the dawning happiness in Emily's eyes.

"Emily," he began aggressively.

"I love you, Jacob. I've loved you for ages. The only reason I got engaged to Brad Carlton was that I thought there was no hope for you and me. I decided I might as well marry him as anyone," Emily admitted. "I didn't think I could ever have you. Later, when you told me you would never marry again I decided to adopt a similar attitude. I made up my mind that if I couldn't have you, I didn't want anyone. Then you went abroad and Grandmother died and I put all my energy into opening Emily's Garden."

"It's selfish as hell of me to say this, but the truth is, sweetheart, I'm very glad you took that vow and I'm very glad you got involved with Emily's Garden instead of another man. That way you were free to come to me when I finally decided to come back. I've loved you for so long, honey."

"Oh, Jacob," she breathed. For the first time that day, her eyes focused on him and him alone. "I loved you, too, right from the beginning, I think, even though you made me so mad at times. I was crushed when I learned you'd gone to work for the foreign operations department. I thought I'd never see you again. Then, when you showed up in my life playing the same old role for my family, I was furious and hurt. It seemed you only came back to interfere with my future again."

"I came back to see what had happened to you, Emily. I had to know if you'd changed. I knew you could never have handled marriage with me two years ago. Your family would have been able to pressure you into leaving me. Or they could have convinced me that I was no good for you. I already believed it myself."

"Jacob, how can you say such things?"

He shrugged. "Because they're true. But I've had two years to put the past behind me. You aren't the only one who's changed, honey. I've decided I'll make you a damned good husband, even with all my previously noted drawbacks."

She gave him a misty smile. "I never doubted it."

"Five years ago things were impossible for us. Two years ago we were both vulnerable in different ways," Jacob said softly. "But things are different now. I've decided I deserve you and as for you—"

"What about me?"

"You've come into your own. You're so much stronger now, Emily." Jacob smiled slightly. "I'm dealing with a full-blown passion flower, not a delicate, budding rose that can be crushed by a high wind or too much rain. I figure this passion flower can make up her own mind about me and stick to her decision. She won't let her family sway her."

Emily shook her head swiftly. "Never, Jacob. I would never let them change my mind about you. They wouldn't have been able to change it before if they had tried. I knew then that I wanted you."

Jacob nestled his face in her sweet-smelling hair. "Maybe I was the one who lacked faith two years ago. Don't make the same mistake now that I made then, Emily. Love me, sweetheart. Love me enough to trust me."

She looked up at him and he saw the flaring emotion in her eyes. He could see her sorting through the myriad hopes and uncertainties that had been plaguing her, and then she seemed to reach a conclusion. For the first time since he had asked her to marry him, she finally relaxed and surrendered to her love. Jacob felt something tight and dangerous unwind within himself at the same time. It was going to be all right, he thought. It was really going to be all right.

"I do love you, Jacob." Her smile was tremulous but very real and it caught at his heart. "And I do trust you. More than anyone else in the world."

He hugged her tightly. "Enough to believe I can handle your family if it comes to that?"

"I think you could handle just about anyone," she said softly. "You once asked me who they could send to intimidate a professional intimidator. I should have listened to you then. You're right. I've let my imagination run wild. My family is ruthless, stubborn and difficult, but—" she grinned "—you're even more so."

"I'll assume that's a compliment," he remarked dryly.

"Oh, it is. But underneath it all, none of you are monsters. It's going to be okay, isn't it?"

Jacob breathed a heavy sigh of relief. "It's going to be just fine." He rocked her gently in his embrace for a long, precious moment. "Everything is going to be fine."

"I can hardly believe this is my wedding night."

"It wasn't much of a wedding," Jacob muttered, feeling guilty for the first time. "But we'll make up for it when we get back to Seattle. We'll throw ourselves a huge reception and you can do all the flowers. How's that?"

She laughed softly. "Whatever you say, Jacob."

"I like a woman who knows when to give in."

"Beast."

Some of the humor went out of him. "I know. And you're Beauty. According to the fairy tale we should make a perfect couple."

"I think you're supposed to turn into a prince somewhere along the line."

"Details, details," he scoffed.

"It's the little things that count in life." Her hands moved over him and she smiled with sweet, enticing wickedness. "But there's nothing about you that's particularly little."

Jacob groaned as he felt her palm brush across the front of his slacks. He bent his head and kissed her forcefully. When she responded instantly, melting against him and parting her lips, the very blood in his veins seemed to roar as it began to heat.

"You're the best thing that ever happened to me, Emily," he confessed thickly. "Maybe that's why I was afraid to take you when you were younger. I didn't really believe anything that good could happen to me. And I'd made such a mess of my first marriage."

She touched his face with infinite compassion. "It's all in the past. Let it stay there. We have our future to think about now."

He willingly shook off the aching feeling of too much time wasted. She was right. What was past, was past. It was time to concentrate on the present and the future.

Jacob gathered her close, the red-and-gold silk sliding under his rough palms as he lovingly shaped the curves and hollows of Emily's slender body. She was so perfect, he thought, and did not stop to question why he should find her so. He accepted on some level deep within himself that she was his true mate and that fact made her perfect. She aroused him more than any other woman he had ever met, and now this perfect mate was his wife. His body was already beginning to scream for release.

"Come to bed and let me love you," he muttered as he found the zipper of the silk dress and fumbled with it.

His hands felt clumsy and awkward, but the dress eventually came undone and fell into a pool of crimson and gold. He carefully removed Emily's glasses and placed them on the side table. As always, taking off her glasses was a strangely intimate gesture that made him feel he was removing some secret veil. Her amber eyes were brilliant and full of a woman's mysteries as she looked up at him.

When her fingers went to the buttons of his shirt, Jacob waited impatiently for her to slip the garment off his shoulders. When she seemed to be taking too long, he finished the job himself. A few minutes later they were both naked, and Jacob was vividly aware of the heavy ache of his own arousal. He bent and scooped Emily up in his arms and carried her to the turned-back bed. He placed her gently on the sheets.

"My wife," he murmured in wonder as he lowered himself beside her. He felt dazed with the knowledge, and as passion flamed into life between them, he gave himself up to the only source of real happiness he had ever known. He would take care of her, he promised himself. He would take very good care of her for as long as he lived.

It amazed him that Emily had actually harbored doubts about his ability to fend off her disapproving family. She ought to realize that he would walk through hell to protect her and the love they had.

10

"I STILL THINK this is a really stupid idea," Emily announced as she reluctantly climbed out of the Mercedes and stood looking doubtfully at her parents' home.

"Wives are supposed to give their husbands lots of moral support. You're supposed to fluff up the male ego and tell him how brilliant and bold he is." Jacob closed the door on his side of the car and walked around the front to collect her.

Emily wrinkled her nose at him. "Where did you get that notion?"

"All men know how wives are supposed to behave. We're born knowing."

"Is that right? It must come as kind of a shock for each new generation of males when they discover that women don't always behave the way they're supposed to, hmm?"

Jacob shook his head mournfully. "It's a shock, all right. But we persevere."

"How optimistic of you." Emily caught hold of his hand as they walked to the front door. "But I still think coming to see my family after only being married for three days was a big mistake. This is our honeymoon. Why should we spoil it?"

"You're just nervous about facing them, that's all."

"Confrontations with my family are not my most favorite way of passing time."

"Calm down," Jacob said soothingly as he rang the doorbell. "There isn't going to be any confrontation. We simply accept their warm congratulations and then we ask what the hell's going on with Morrell and the Fowler deal."

"In that order?"

"Sure. Why not?"

"Well, for one thing—" Emily began, and then stopped abruptly as the door opened. The Ravenscrofts' middle-aged housekeeper smiled at her.

"Hello, Emily. Good to see you again. Come on in. You, too, Mr. Stone. The family is expecting you. They're all in the garden room."

"Thanks, Myra. We know the way," Emily murmured.

"You'll be staying for dinner?" Myra asked.

"No," said Emily.

"Yes," Jacob said simultaneously.

Myra glanced from one to the other. "Well, which is it?"

Jacob grinned. "We'll be staying unless we're thrown out. That's about all I can tell you at the moment. But knowing the Ravenscrofts, I think you can count on feeding us."

Myra chuckled. "I think so, too. They won't let either of you get away too quickly." She arched an eyebrow at Emily. "Especially you, young lady. You've managed to throw the whole family into a tizzy again. Not for the first time, I might add. But don't worry about it. It's good for them. They would all have become completely over-bearing and incredibly dull years ago if it hadn't been for you. You keep them on their toes and a little off balance. They need that. The rest of the world runs too much their way most of the time. See you at dinner."

Emily watched Myra head for the kitchen and then turned to Jacob. "Well? Are you ready? We might as well get this over with."

"Relax. You're not going to your execution. I'll handle everything."

Emily groaned. "I can't believe you're being so casual about this."

"You think this is the worst thing I've ever walked into?" Jacob asked quietly.

Emily frowned, thinking about it. "Probably not," she admitted at last. "How do you do it, Jacob? How can you be so cool and strong in a crisis? I envy you."

"I got my assertiveness training on the job," he explained laconically. He paused and then added, "Myra's right, you know."

"About what?"

"About you being good for your family. You're good for me, too. You may have turned us all prematurely gray, but you'll keep us from becoming too complacent and set in our ways. Things are never dull around you, sweetheart."

Emily grinned for the first time that afternoon. "That's the amazing thing about nature, isn't it. There's a role, no matter how minor, for every living creature, even us mosquitoes."

Jacob stopped at the entrance to the glass-walled garden room that lined the back of the Ravenscroft home. He pulled Emily into his arms and kissed her with quick, rough passion. "You're not a mosquito. You're a sexy little passion flower, and your role in my life is not minor. You're the most important thing that ever happened to me."

Emily walked into the tiled garden room, flushed with the aftermath of Jacob's kiss and the sweet satisfaction of knowing she was loved. At that moment, she felt certain she could face anything, even a bunch of Ravenscrofts.

And they were all there to put her certainty to the test.

"Darling!" Catherine exclaimed, moving forward to hug her daughter. "What a surprise you've given us. We had no idea you were planning marriage. How could you keep it a secret? We're all in shock."

Emily smiled wryly. "Now, Mother, we all know it takes a lot more than an unexpected marriage to shock a true Ravenscroft."

"Hello, Jacob," Drake said with a welcoming grin. He held out a hand, which Jacob shook without hesitation. "Congratulations. Now she's your problem."

"Drake!" Catherine admonished. "What a thing to say."

Gifford Ravenscroft nodded coolly at his new son-in-law, his gaze speculative. "I always did say your greatest asset, Stone, was the fact that no one around you ever really knew for certain what you were thinking. You moved quickly this time, didn't you?"

Jacob smiled faintly, his eyes as watchful as those of his former employer. "Not really. I've been waiting for Emily for a long time."

There was an uncomfortable hush as everyone absorbed the meaning of that, and then Drake broke the uneasy silence to ask Jacob and Emily what they wanted to drink. After that, Catherine, with the automatic skills of a good hostess, managed to find a more neutral topic.

Of all the people in the room, Emily thought, her brother seemed to be enjoying himself the most. It was as if he was secretly very amused by the whole event. When he caught Emily's eye, Drake winked reassuringly.

A few minutes later when he handed her the glass of wine he had poured for her, he said in a low voice that reached her alone, "Take it easy. Stone's been in worse situations than this."

Emily's eyes widened, and then she chuckled. "That's what he told me. But I can't help it. My stomach is tied in a knot."

"Take a couple of sips of the wine," Drake advised before he moved off to refill his mother's drink.

Emily followed his advice and then sat down in an antique wicker chair. It was a relief to get off her feet. Jacob, who had been politely talking to her mother, took a chair near Emily, a glass of Scotch in his fist. He glanced first at Drake and then at Gifford.

"What's been happening with Morrell?"

Gifford's eyes narrowed thoughtfully. "It's under control."

Drake nodded. "We signed the papers on the Fowler deal yesterday. Morrell knows he's out of the running on that project. It's too late for him to try anything underhanded." Drake shot a quick, hooded glance at his sister.

Emily pointedly ignored him and sipped her wine.

"I assume you followed that up with a little insurance?" Jacob inquired dryly.

Drake nodded. "I followed that lead you gave me and did some research on the Satterly deal. You were right. Morrell was walking a very shaky line on that one. That stock was bouncing all over the place when he started buying it. He had to have been using inside information. It wouldn't take much work to turn up some concrete evidence to turn over to the Securities Exchange Commission. I discreetly let Morrell know RI was willing to go to the trouble of investigating his connection with Satterly ourselves if he gave us any more problems. He's not stupid. He knows when he's beaten."

"Do you really think he sent those punks after Jacob?" Emily asked, still unable to believe the Damon she had known would sink to that level.

Drake shrugged. "We'll never know for sure. It could have been a simple case of attempted assault and robbery. We can only be grateful it was Jacob who drove into the garage at that particular moment and not you. We told you when you rented that apartment that the garage looked dangerous."

Emily made a face at him which Drake ignored. He continued his summary of events, his eyes on Jacob. "Morrell sure as hell played innocent. But I let him know we had our suspicions about that garage incident and that we did not want to see any more unfortunate coincidences happening to any member of the family or to any of our friends. I warned him that we would use the Satterly deal to bring down his whole empire if anything happened. He'll watch his step now."

"Reassuring," Jacob commented blandly as he took another swallow of his drink.

"A pack of wolves," Emily murmured almost to herself.

"What was that, dear?" Catherine asked.

"Nothing. I was just making a general comment on the ways of big business."

Jacob looked at her. "You have to be able to defend your own, honey, or you and yours will get trampled. Just because we're not living in the jungle any longer doesn't mean the law of survival of the fittest has been repealed."

"Grandmother always said it was possible to conduct good business and maintain good ethical standards at the same time," Emily said.

Jacob shrugged. "She was right. For the most part. But sometimes you have to fight and when you do, you use whatever weapons you've got."

"I'm afraid Grandmother Ravenscroft was something of an idealist," Catherine said sadly. "She was very noble and high-minded about things, but she didn't always understand the business world."

"There's something I would like to know," Emily continued. Everyone looked at her. "Why was Damon so determined to beat you on the Fowler deal, and why did he want to hurt RI? Why was he looking for revenge?"

"I told you, it's just an old business score he wants to settle," Gifford assured her mildly.

Emily met her father's gaze. "I want to know the truth."

Her parents stared at her, clearly surprised by her insistence. But apparently they were getting accustomed to their daughter's new brand of assertiveness.

"Well," Gifford explained slowly, "it goes back to a big project down in South America that was put out for bid a couple of years ago. Morrell's people thought they had it all sewed up, but we decided to take a shot at it. We got lucky because of some contacts we had made on a previous operation down there. In South America, as in most other places around the world, it isn't necessarily the low bid that wins. It's who you know in government and industry that counts. RI has excellent contacts in South America. When we put those together with a bid that was more or less on a par with Morrell's, we got the job."

"It was just another business deal to us," Drake said. "But Morrell took it personally. He swore at the time he would get even, but we figured he was just letting off steam. Until we found out a few months ago that he had started seeing you, that is. Then we knew he was up to something and he intended to use you to get it."

"You decided the something he was after had to be a chunk of RI, right?" Emily tapped one nail on the arm of her chair. "You just assumed that because the man had started dating me that he intended to marry me so he could control those shares. Without any real evidence, you took it for granted he was up to no good."

"Emily," Jacob interrupted mildly, "calm down. They assumed right and you know it. Morrell admitted as much that day he came to your apartment."

"That's not the point," Emily declared, warming to her theme, "it's the way everyone instantly jumped to the conclusion that I and my precious shares needed to be protected that irritates me."

"Emily," Jacob tried again, his voice still mild, "you did need protection."

"I did not," she announced baldly. "I never in a million years would have married Damon Morrell. He was only a casual date as far as I was concerned. But no one bothered to ask for my side of the situation before jumping all over me with hobnail boots. Oh, no, you all leaped to the conclusion that I was in imminent danger of marrying. Not only that, you all assumed that if I did marry, I would automatically turn the RI shares over to Damon as if it were some sort of dowry. Well, I've got news for you. I would never have done that. I couldn't turn those shares over to someone outside the family, even if I wanted to. In fact, I can't even sell them to someone outside the family."

She had their attention now. They were all watching her in stunned amazement.

"What do you mean, you couldn't give or sell those shares, Emily?" Drake finally asked.

Emily smiled grimly. "Grandmother gave me those shares on her deathbed, but what no one here knew was that there were a few strings attached. Remember how she called me in and spoke to me alone the night before she died?"

"I remember," Catherine said with a small frown.

"She told me then that one day I would assume the role she was relinquishing."

"She saw herself as the company's corporate conscience," Gifford said slowly. "She didn't interfere often, but when she did she was as stubborn as all hell."

"Exactly," Emily agreed. "I hate to break this to all of you, but I'm afraid she selected me to take her place. She said I would eventually have to become RI's conscience. Ravenscrofts were born hunters, she said, and they were very good at what they did. They knew how to survive. But she felt they occasionally needed someone to pull on the leash. She gave me enough shares and enough potential power in RI to do that if it ever became necessary. I told her I didn't think I could handle it. I reminded her that I always seem to lose when I go up against the rest of you. But she said that someday things would be different. She said I was her granddaughter and she knew me. She said I just needed time."

"Emily," Catherine said weakly, "this is incredible. Why haven't you ever said anything about this before?"

Emily shrugged. "She told me to bide my time and wait until I felt confident before I tried flexing any muscle. She said I needed to grow and mature but that at some point in the future I would be ready to handle the job. She made me promise never to sell or give away my shares unless the family sold the firm outright. As long as Ravenscrofts run RI, I have to retain possession of those shares and I have to keep my seat on the board. She said she was entrusting the future of the family and the firm to me."

Gifford shook his head in wry disgust. "The incredible part is I can just see her doing something like that. She was a magnificent, interfering, arrogant old lady."

"Someday I hope to be just like her," Emily said complacently.

Jacob groaned but there was laughter in his eyes. "I have a feeling we've all just seen a vision of the future."

"What about the night you threatened us with those shares if we didn't leave Jacob alone, Emily?" Catherine asked.

"A bluff, I'm afraid," Emily said with a sigh. "I could never get rid of those damned shares. I gave Grandmother my word of honor. But I thought I'd try pulling off a true Ravenscroft maneuver with them. Unfortunately," she added with a sidelong glance at Jacob, "someone else stepped in and nipped my big plans in the bud."

"Who was that?" Gifford demanded.

"Jacob. He didn't like the idea of me trying to protect him."

"Do you mean to say that you are now going to start taking an active interest in the day-to-day operations of RI?" Drake asked without undue concern.

"Nope. I have absolutely no interest in the day-to-day running of the company," Emily assured him. "I'll just be keeping tabs on things from afar. Grandmother made it clear that she considered you the best candidate for the job of actually directing RI's daily activities. She said you had the necessary predatory qualities to keep the firm alive and aggressive."

"I wonder if she meant that as a compliment," Drake said wryly.

"Oh, yes, she did," Emily said quite earnestly, remembering her grandmother's final words. "She said you had inherited all the necessary traits to make the firm thrive and grow and to protect it for the next generation. But she felt strongly that the company needed someone in the background who could step in occasionally and remind the board of directors about the difference between right and wrong. It was Grandmother's opinion that just knowing there was someone ready to interfere at a moment's notice would be enough to keep the firm from straying too far into the shadows. She recognized the fine line between good business and what was morally wrong even if it was legal."

"And she expected you to monitor that line?" Gifford asked bluntly.

"I'm afraid so," Emily said cheerfully, beginning to enjoy herself.

Drake stared at his sister for a long moment. Then he turned to Jacob. "Did you know what you were getting into when you carried her off to Reno?"

Jacob's teeth flashed briefly in a dangerous grin, but his eyes were warm and indulgent when he looked at Emily. "I've told Emily more than once that she needs a keeper. But now I'm starting to wonder if it isn't the rest of us who will need protection."

Drake smiled. "You may be right. Speaking of protection, I found dealing directly with Morrell an interesting experience. It made me realize what you used to go through for RI on a routine basis whenever we sent you out to tackle someone like him."

"That's why I let you do it," Jacob said. "I figured you might as well get used to handling the dirty work yourself because I'm not going to be available to handle it for you in the future."

Catherine eyed him sharply, but her tone was deceptively polite as she asked sharply, "You're not planning to ask for your old job back now that you're married to Emily?"

"Marrying Emily doesn't change my personal plans. One of the reasons I resigned in the first place was because I didn't want to be in the position of marrying the boss's sister." He raised his glass in a half-mocking salute to Drake. "Or the daughter of the other two members of the board." He nodded at Gifford and Catherine.

"You mean you knew when you came back to the States two months ago that you were going to marry Emily?" Catherine looked shocked.

"I knew I was going to do everything in my power to marry her," Jacob said calmly.

Drake smiled slightly but said nothing. He looked as if he'd just had a private suspicion confirmed. Gifford shifted in his chair, narrowed his eyes and took a long swallow of his drink.

"I see," Catherine said tightly. "Just what are you going to be doing in the future, then, Jacob?"

Jacob glanced at Emily, his eyes unexpectedly warm. "I'm not sure yet, but I have a hunch Emily and I will be moving soon."

Emily nearly choked on her wine. She opened her mouth to ask him what he meant by that, but before she could get the question out, her mother already had.

"Moving where?" Catherine demanded.

"Arizona, I think," Jacob said musingly. "But it's not certain yet. I can open my consulting firm almost anywhere, but we'll need to find a place where Emily can start a new flower shop."

Gifford Ravenscroft glared at Jacob. "Why is it necessary to move?"

Jacob grinned. "It isn't absolutely necessary but it occurred to me that a little distance might be beneficial."

Drake chuckled. "You mean a little distance between us and you and Emily?"

"I knew you'd understand," Jacob said politely.

Catherine started to protest. Gifford watched Jacob like a hawk, and Emily decided this might be a very good time to keep her mouth shut. Jacob had said he would handle this little scene, and he certainly seemed intent on doing it his way.

It was Gifford who made the decisive move. He took command of the situation by simply clearing his throat. Everyone turned to look at him.

"So you're going to go through with this consulting business idea, Jacob?"

"It's either that or accept Emily's offer of employment. She's told me she would hire me full-time to deliver flowers. Actually, it's not a bad offer. The work is interesting, you meet some nice people and the tips are good."

Drake growled his laughter and immediately tried to muffle his amusement with a swallow from his glass of whiskey. His eyes met Emily's over the rim of his glass, and she knew exactly what he was thinking. The image of Jacob delivering flowers was more than a little outrageous.

"The funny thing is," she said softly, "he's really very good at it."

"Is that right?" Drake gave Jacob a speculative glance.

Gifford glared at his new son-in-law. "Forget the jokes about delivering flowers. You'll need a stake to get started in the consulting business."

"Will I?" Jacob asked politely.

Emily's complacency faded abruptly. She sensed danger. She had lived with this family too long not to recognize the signs.

"If you want to be competitive right from the start, you'll need at least a hundred thousand just for first-year expenses. Possibly a hundred and fifty. Office space, staff, traveling expenses—they all add up in a hurry. Getting through the first year is the easy part. The second year is the toughest. You'll probably need an additional source of funds to survive the second eighteen months in business. After that, if you're lucky, you might be running in the black. That's assuming everything clicks, and that you find enough clients to keep you afloat."

"I've learned a lot watching how Ravenscroft International works," Jacob said calmly.

"We paid you well, but I doubt we paid you enough to enable you to start up a major consulting firm from scratch," Gifford declared.

"I've been able to save a few bucks," Jacob said easily.

Emily shifted uneasily in her chair as she realized where all this was leading. Her fingers tightened on the wicker arms. Drake seemed unperturbed by it all. He was watching the other two men as if he still found something vastly amusing. Catherine was looking anxiously at her daughter and back at her husband.

"You're going to have to plan on something in the neighborhood of a quarter of a million, Stone," Gifford said bluntly. "You might as well be realistic about this. It costs money to go into business these days, especially the kind of business you're planning on opening. The competition is tough."

"Like I said, I've learned a lot watching RI operate."

Gifford swirled the ice cubes in his glass and then smoothly fired his big guns. "I think that we might be able to negotiate a deal, Stone. I'm willing to loan you the two hundred and fifty at no interest under certain circumstances."

Emily went very still. She knew what those circumstances were. Gifford was going to offer a deal which would undoubtedly involve Jacob filing for divorce in exchange for a quarter of a million dollars that he could use to start his new business. Her knuckles went white around her glass.

She wanted to leap to her feet and scream her protest, but in that moment she caught Jacob's eye and the angry, impassioned words died on her lips. Jacob watched her sink back into herself, and his mouth curved faintly. He turned to Gifford and spoke deliberately.

"Gifford, I've worked for you long enough to know that the last thing in the world I would ever do is allow you to invest in my business. No offense, but we both know that the kind of offer you're making comes with a lot of strings attached. I don't have any intention of letting myself get tangled up in strings of any kind, especially not the kind pulled by a Ravenscroft."

Gifford watched him for a long moment. "I believe you really mean that."

"You, of all people, should know Jacob never says anything he doesn't mean," Drake pointed out. He glanced at his watch. "I think it's time for dinner. Shall we go? You know how Myra hates to be kept waiting."

Gifford shot his son a quick look. "The rest of you go on. Jacob and I will be along shortly."

Catherine got to her feet at once and so did Drake.

"Coming, Emily?" Catherine asked pointedly.

Emily hesitated, and then she smiled at her husband. "Why not?" she murmured. "Jacob can take care of himself."

Jacob caught her hand as she walked past his chair and squeezed her fingers reassuringly. "Thanks for the vote of confidence," he said too softly for the others to hear.

She smiled at him again and then went to join her mother and Drake. The three of them left the room.

"I just can't believe it," Catherine said bluntly out in the hall. "How could you take us by surprise like this, Emily? First the marriage and then this news about your private agreement with Grandmother Ravenscroft. It's too much. What has gotten into you lately? You never used to do things like this."

"Correction," Drake said lightly. "She used to try doing things like this in the past. She just didn't get away with them until recently. Our sweet little Emily has finally blossomed into full flower, I'm afraid. And it was Jacob Stone who was around to pick the blossom when it was ready. The man always did have an uncanny sense of timing."

"I know this is probably going to come as a shock to you, Mom, but I've loved Jacob Stone since the day he rescued me from that deranged kidnapper," Emily said gently.

"You what?" Catherine was totally nonplussed.

"It's true. But he was married then and I assumed there was no future for us. Even after his divorce I never dared to hope he might love me in return until you and Dad kindly brought him back into my life a few weeks ago. How can I ever thank you?"

Drake chuckled as Catherine glared at her daughter. "Don't worry, Mom, it wasn't really your fault. Stone came back looking for Emily. He would have found her on his own. I realized that a while ago. It was just sheer coincidence we asked him to give us a hand getting her away from Morrell. By the time he got back to the States he had officially resigned from RI. Didn't you wonder why he agreed so readily to help us get Emily out of the situation with Morrell?"

"We trusted that man!" Catherine exclaimed. "We trusted him for years. How could he do this to us?"

"I'd like to point out," Emily said firmly, "that I had a hand in the decision. I married him because I love him and because I know he loves me. Furthermore, I think he's right. I believe it would be best if we moved to Arizona. Or maybe Florida."

"Emily, for heaven's sake, don't talk like that," Catherine snapped. "Why would you want to live so far away from your family?"

Emily grinned. "I'll give you one guess."

Her mother sighed. "You've always resented what you call our interference, haven't you?"

"It has been a bit wearing at times," Emily said as she sat down at the dining room table. "You've never given me any credit for being able to look after myself."

"We only wanted what was best for you, dear," Catherine said earnestly.

"And what was best for RI, too, naturally."

"The well-being of the members of this family has always been tied to the well-being of the company. You seem to have developed a very sharp tongue lately," Catherine observed.

Drake looked at his sister as he sat down across from her. "Probably that assertiveness training class she took."

"Or," said Emily thoughtfully, "it could just be that I've finally grown up and become a real Ravenscroft, just as Grandmother promised I would."

"Now there's a thought to freeze the blood in one's veins," Drake remarked.

Catherine glared at him. "I don't see how you can take this so lightly, Drake. But I assure you it isn't finished yet. We'll wait and see what happens after Gifford talks to Jacob privately."

Emily smiled serenely, aware of the depths of her own newfound confidence in the man she loved. Something deep inside her relaxed. "Nothing will change, Mother. I think you had better resign yourself to the inevitable."

Catherine studied her daughter for a long moment. Then her gaze softened. "You really do love him, don't you?"

"I really love him."

"He'd better take very good care of you," Catherine said finally. "Or he'll have all of us to answer to."

"For the last time," Emily said grimly, "I can take care of myself. Why doesn't anyone around here believe me?"

Before Drake or his mother could come up with an answer, Gifford and Jacob walked into the dining room. Emily searched their faces. Gifford looked stern, but not hostile. Jacob appeared relaxed and totally at ease. He stopped by Emily's chair and dropped a quick, proprietary kiss on her nose.

"The inquisition is over," he announced as he sat down beside her. "Now we can eat. Nothing like facing a bunch of Ravenscrofts to work up a man's appetite."

IT WAS MUCH LATER that night before Emily finally found herself alone with Jacob in the bedroom her mother had assigned them. She turned on her husband as soon as he closed the door.

"Okay, tell me everything. What did my father say to you when he had you alone in the garden room? I warn you I want to hear every last little detail, Jacob."

Jacob loosened his tie with obvious relief and smiled cryptically. "What do you think he said?"

"I want you to tell me. Now."

"Wow. Listen to the woman. '*Now.*' When a female like you starts discovering her own power, there's no stopping her. You're turning into a very arrogant lady, Mrs. Stone."

Emily grinned recklessly. "That's okay. I'm married to a very arrogant man. Grandmother always said that one day I'd learn to hold my own. Tell me what Dad said to you."

Jacob's expression turned into one of wicked humor. "He said I'd better take good care of you or I'd find myself dealing with a whole nest of mad Ravenscrofts."

"Is that all?" Emily demanded in relief. "No more attempts at bribery?"

"Nope."

"No subtle threats?"

"Nope."

"No lectures on how it would be best for me if you got a divorce?"

"Nope."

"No appeals to your former sense of loyalty to RI?"

"Nope."

"Well?" she prompted. "What did you say in response?"

Jacob lightly slung his tie around her neck and tugged her toward him. He held her captive with the strip of silk as he said deliberately, "I told him I'd been taking care of you off and on for a long time and I saw no reason to stop now. In fact, I said I thought I'd be able to do a much more efficient job of it in the future since you're going to be so conveniently close at hand."

"Is that right?" she asked breathlessly.

"That is very right, Emily Ravenscroft Stone." He lowered his head and captured her mouth before Emily could ask any more questions.

THREE DAYS LATER Emily untangled herself from a still-sleeping Jacob, yawned, sat up and prepared to get ready for work. She glanced around her white-on-white room and wondered if she would miss the apartment when the time came to move to Arizona.

Seattle had been good to her and she loved the town, but Jacob was right. It wouldn't do any harm to move a bit beyond her family's immediate reach for a few years. Emily grimaced as she traipsed into the bathroom. Maybe for the rest of her life. Ravenscrofts were okay in small doses, but in larger quantities they were definitely overwhelming.

"What's for breakfast?" Jacob's voice was muffled by his pillow.

"The same thing we had yesterday morning. Cereal."

"Why does it have to be cereal every morning?"

"You're used to eating something better in the mornings?" Emily challenged from the bathroom doorway.

"You used to fix me pancakes and ham and eggs and waffles and stuff."

"We're married now," she reminded him lightly.

"I knew it. I knew that if I married you, you'd start taking me for granted. You haven't even been bringing me coffee in bed lately."

Emily lifted her eyes ceilingward. "Complaints already. Ham and eggs and pancakes and waffles are bad for you on a regular basis."

"Are you sure?"

"Positive."

"Damn."

"And as for coffee in bed, I'm afraid that's only for special occasions. You could, of course, bring me coffee in bed some morning."

Jacob smiled benignly and stretched. "Maybe I'll try that one of these days."

"You do that. In the meantime, you'll have to excuse me. I've got to get ready for work. Careful you don't get so accustomed to the leisure life that you decide to pursue it as a full-time job," Emily warned with a chuckle. She turned to go into the bathroom.

"Emily!"

Startled by the unexpected harshness in his voice, she whirled around. "What is it?"

He swung his feet over the edge of the bed and stalked toward her. His body was strong and hard and lean in the early light, and he was totally unself-conscious about his unsubtle masculine power. "Does it worry you?" he demanded a little roughly.

"Does what worry me?"

"The fact that I'm technically unemployed?"

She stared at him for an instant and then ran forward to throw her arms around him. "What a stupid thing to say. Of course it doesn't worry me. I was just teasing you, Jacob."

He twisted his hands in her hair. "Everything's in place, honey. I didn't feel like going into a lot of detail in front of your parents the other night but you've got a right to know that my plan to open a consulting firm isn't exactly a daydream."

"I never thought it was." She inhaled the unique male scent of him, remembering his ardent lovemaking during the night.

"I guess I've been so busy helping you get ready to sell the shop and making plans to move that I forgot to mention my own financial situation isn't as bad as your father thinks. I told him and the rest of your family that I'd learned a lot watching Ravenscrofts operate over the years. It's true. And a lot of what I learned had to do with investing both here and abroad. I've got the stake I need to get started, Emily."

She smiled against his chest. "And when I sell Emily's Garden I'll have the stake I need to open a new shop down in Arizona. We're going to do just fine, Jacob."

"I know," he agreed. "Just as well because we definitely won't be accepting any help from your family. Now or ever."

"Agreed," she said willingly enough. "You're right, of course. There's no such thing as string-free Ravenscroft help. I just hope that I'll be able to fulfill Grandmother's wishes from a distance. It might be hard to keep an eye on RI operations from Arizona."

"No, it won't," Jacob said with great certainty. "In this day and age, it's possible to keep an eye on a company like RI from almost anywhere on the globe. We'll manage just fine from Arizona. Don't forget, you're still on the board of directors. Technically, they have to keep you informed. All you have to do is insist they do so. Even if they tried a few slick maneuvers without your knowledge, they'd have trouble getting them past you."

"Why?"

"Because you've got me to play guard dog. I've worked for RI so long that I know exactly how your brother and the rest of them operate. I'll warn you if things look odd."

Emily grinned. "Did I ever tell you that Grandmother Ravenscroft always liked you?"

"No, I don't believe you mentioned it. What did the old witch have to say about me?"

"She said she thought you would be good husband material for me."

Jacob looked properly astounded. "You're kidding. She said that?"

"I'm afraid so," Emily said cheerfully. "I, of course, told her she was crazy. You had left for one of the foreign offices two months before and I just knew I'd never see you again. But she said she had a hunch you'd be back one day."

"Well, how about that?" Jacob was smugly pleased. "I did get some Ravenscroft approval, after all."

"I guess you could say that."

He lifted her chin and kissed her soundly. "Umm, you taste good."

"That's true love for you. I haven't even brushed my teeth yet this morning."

"Let's go back to bed," Jacob suggested huskily.

Emily shook her head regretfully. "You know I can't do that. I've got too much to do to get the shop ready for sale."

"I know." He released her reluctantly. "I'll drop by around lunchtime, okay?"

"It's a deal."

Half an hour later Emily hastily finished the last of her cereal and grabbed her oversize shoulder bag. "Got to run." She bent down to kiss Jacob goodbye. He was drinking his coffee in a leisurely manner, enjoying the morning paper that had arrived a short while earlier. Emily felt a thrill of pleasure at the very settled, very married feeling the whole scene engendered in her. Life seemed very good that morning.

"See you at lunchtime," Jacob said, darting his tongue along her lower lip in an intimate, teasing gesture.

He watched her hurry toward the door where she paused briefly on the threshold to wave to him. Then he glanced at his watch and gave her two minutes to catch the elevator. When he was certain she was out of the hall and on her way down to the garage, he got to his feet and pocketed his set of keys.

When he opened the front door of the apartment he found the corridor empty, just as he had expected. Having followed Emily down to the garage every morning since their return, he had perfected the timing.

Jacob sauntered down to the elevator and stabbed the call button. Emily would be furious if she knew he had made it a policy to escort her, unseen, to the garage every day. She was getting extremely prickly lately about being taken care of.

But Jacob's memory of the two punks who had been waiting for him in the garage had permanently shaped his attitude toward Emily's safety in the building. He had no intention of letting her come and go alone in that dungeon downstairs.

So far she hadn't questioned the fact that he always met her after work at the shop and drove home with her. Jacob smiled to himself as the elevator door opened on the lower garage level, and he stepped out. If she realized his main reason for doing it was to prevent her from having to drive into the garage alone, she would probably tear a wide strip off him.

The best way to take care of Emily was with discretion, Jacob had discovered. He was quite proud of himself for figuring that out. Her family had gone about it the wrong way since the day she was born and he himself had more than once been guilty of too forthright an approach. Much simpler to keep an eye on her from a discreet distance.

Jacob stayed out of sight in the elevator lobby. He was always careful to make certain he didn't go into the main parking area where Emily would spot him on her way out. From here he would be able to hear her car and watch the iron gate open and close.

Discretion, he told himself. No need to be heavy-handed about it. A husband had to learn subtlety in dealing with a wife.

He was congratulating himself on his skill when he heard Damon Morrell's voice. Jacob recognized it instantly. Morrell was on the other side of the lobby wall, speaking in a harsh, angry tone. Simultaneously Jacob registered the fact that Emily had not yet started her car.

Jacob's vow of discretion crumpled into nothingness. Instinctively he started to launch himself around the corner, his hands already anticipating the feel of Morrell's throat. And then, before he came into sight of the other two, Jacob forced himself to a shuddering halt.

He was never really certain what made him stop. It had something to do with the fact that Emily's voice was calm and controlled, with no trace of alarm. That quiet control made him remember how angry she had been the last time he had stepped in to "rescue" her from Morrell. She had been so resentful of the implication that she couldn't take care of herself, Jacob recalled wryly.

He took a deep, calming breath, aware of the adrenaline pounding through him. It was all right, he told himself. He could tell by the sound of her voice that she was in no immediate danger. He should let her handle this. She would undoubtedly be furious if he stepped in again, uninvited.

Jacob leaned against the partition that separated him from Emily and Morrell and made himself stay where he was. He could monitor the situation from there. If Morrell turned nasty, there would be plenty of time to move in on him. Jacob gritted his teeth and swore he would give Emily her chance to handle the man.

Emily had been so astonished to see Damon waiting for her near her car that she nearly dropped her keys.

"What on earth are you doing here?" she demanded.

Morrell watched her through hooded eyes, his hands shoved deep into the pockets of his fashionable jacket. "It was the only way I could think of to see you alone. I've been watching you for three days, waiting to find you alone. That damned husband of yours hardly lets you out of his sight. When you're not with him, you're at the shop with Diane and a bunch of customers."

"How would you know what I'm doing with my time these days, Damon?" Something in his eyes made Emily wary. She kept her distance, not going any closer to the car.

"I told you, I've been keeping an eye on you."

"Why, Damon?"

"You have a lot of nerve asking a stupid question like that." Damon's voice didn't rise, but there was a savage rawness in it that told its own story. "You've ruined everything. You know that, don't you?"

"If you're talking about what happened between you and RI over that Fowler deal—"

"That was only part of it. But it was a big part. I should have had that project, Emily. It should have been mine. I needed it badly to cover some recent losses. RI stole it from me. This isn't the first time they've stolen something from me."

"Come off it, Damon, we both know how business is done these days. You play just as rough as RI does. If you'd had the right contacts down in South America you would have used them, just as you used your friends in the Middle East last year to secure that airport project. I had nothing to do with your winning or losing, and I don't want to have anything to do with it. The truth is,

I don't like the way international business is done and I prefer to be left out of it entirely."

Damon stared at her, his eyes hot with repressed fury. "If I had married you, everything would have been different. I would have had RI right where I wanted it. I could have controlled the company through you. Do you know what I was going to force your family to do, Emily? I was going to make them merge with my company. I was going to create the most powerful construction firm in the Northwest, maybe on the whole West Coast, and in the process, RI would have effectively ceased to exist."

Emily caught her breath, realizing at last the extent of his frustrated anger. "You were willing to use me to break RI and to build your own firm into this superpower?"

"You were the key, Emily. I realized that months ago when I found out you were living here in Seattle. I knew then what I had to do. It was so easy at first. I had you eating out of the palm of my hand."

"Damon, for heaven's sake, we never even went to bed together," Emily protested, thoroughly exasperated. "How can you imply a serious relationship? I've told you before that I considered us casual friends, that's all. I resent the fact that you think you could have married me."

"I could have had you if that bastard Stone hadn't arrived on the scene."

"Not a chance." Emily was infuriated. "We've already been through this. Why does everyone and his brother think I'm a chunk of clay he can mold to his own purpose? Believe it or not, I have a few personal goals myself. I am not as malleable as everyone seems to think."

Damon did not appear to hear her. He was too involved in rehashing what he thought he had lost. "You were no problem. I had you under control. It was Stone and your family who screwed it all up. I guess your family figured it was safer to have you married to him than me."

"You're crazy, Damon."

"You think so? You're the one who's out of her mind if you really think you're making your own decisions these days. I did a little research on Jacob Stone. He's RI's man right to the core. He'll do whatever your family tells him to do, up to and including marrying you. When your people started getting nervous about the fact that you were seeing me, they took steps to pick out a nice safe husband for you. How does it feel to be married off to someone your family can control, Emily?"

"You've got it all wrong, Damon," she whispered.

He shook his head once. "No, I've finally figured it all out. I tried to scare Stone off, but things went wrong."

"It *was* you who sent those two thugs after him here in my garage that night, wasn't it?" Emily was genuinely shocked at the realization. "Jacob and my family had their suspicions, but until now I didn't really believe them. I thought I knew you well enough to bet you wouldn't have stooped to such a thing. How dare you, Damon? How dare you pull a cowardly trick like that?"

"Cut the drama. It was worth a try. I'd had those two watching your garage since Stone first appeared on the scene. Hell, I had them in place right after you got back from Portland. I knew something was up. I just wasn't sure what or how to deal with it. I finally decided to make a move on Stone. I decided to see if he could be scared off. But things went wrong. Dammit, Emily, I was so close! I almost had you, and with you I would have had RI. You've ruined everything!"

He reached for her without any warning.

It happened so quickly that Emily did not even have time to think. In a matter of seconds the argument had gone from a shouting match straight into outright violence.

She felt his fingers close around her arm and knew he was going to jerk her off her feet. This time he wasn't just trying to force a kiss on her. This time Damon was going to hurt her. There was no time to reflect on the subject. Emily acted without conscious planning.

She leaned into the direction he was pulling, throwing Damon off balance because he had been expecting resistance and was braced for it.

As he staggered a bit, readjusting his weight, Emily pushed against his opposite shoulder and simultaneously hooked a foot around his ankle.

Completely off balance, Morrell went sprawling. He shouted something as he reeled back against the car and tried to catch himself by grabbing at the side mirror. The mirror bent, offering no support, and Damon hit the concrete.

Emily did not stick around to gloat. She whirled and began to dash around the corner of the lobby wall, heading for the elevators.

She was halfway to her goal when she collided with Jacob's massive frame as he came charging around the partition.

The impact took away Emily's breath. His big hands caught her and steadied her for an instant. Her dazed eyes flew to his face. She had time to register the cold granite of his features and then he was putting her aside, getting her out of the way so that he could reach Morrell.

"I told you what I'd do the next time I found you bothering Emily, Morrell." Jacob leaned down and grabbed a fistful of the other man's jacket, jerking Damon to his feet. Jacob cocked one arm, his hand knotting into a fist.

"Jacob, wait!" Emily finally came to her senses. "There's no need to hit him. I don't want any unnecessary violence."

Jacob didn't look at her. His eyes were savagely intent on his victim, who was staring at him groggily. "What do you expect me to do? Shake his hand?"

"I expect you to call the cops like a good citizen," Emily said firmly. "I mean it, Jacob, this has gone far enough. I will not have you meting out your own brand of justice."

Jacob did glance at her then, his expression unreadable. "You want the cops? Go call 'em," he suggested innocently.

Emily nodded warily and turned toward the elevators. Then she paused. "You promise you won't beat him up while I'm gone?"

"Now, why would I want to do that? You've already decked him once. Emily, if you're not going to go upstairs and call the cops, we might as well break out a pack of cards and play gin. Make up your mind."

Emily gave him one last warning glance and then put her key into the elevator call lock.

Jacob waited until the elevator closed and then he smiled at Damon in wolfish anticipation. "I'll bet you had no idea how dangerous these underground parking garages can be, Morrell. Well, live and learn. I'm going to show you just how risky it is to hang around one."

EMILY DID NOT get a chance to really talk to Jacob until that evening. After dealing with the police, she had gone straight in to work and the rest of the day had been spent telling Diane the story, dealing with a real estate broker who had a potential client for the shop and selling a great many flowers. By five Emily had had it. She was ready to put her feet up and enjoy a glass of wine.

Jacob wandered into the shop right on time, chatted briefly with Diane and then escorted Emily out to her compact. He took the keys from her and got behind the wheel.

"What a day," Emily muttered as she collapsed against the front seat.

"You sure know how to wake a man up in the morning, I'll give you that," Jacob retorted.

"Don't blame me for that little scene in the garage. If you hadn't followed me downstairs, you would never have gotten involved. I had everything under control." Emily scowled as a thought struck her. "Come to think of it, why *did* you follow me downstairs this morning? I meant to ask you after the police left, but we didn't get a chance to talk. How did you happen to be there when I ran into Damon? Did you think I had forgotten something?"

Jacob concentrated on fighting his way through the evening traffic. "Something like that," he said vaguely.

Emily blinked suspiciously. "What was it?"

"What was what?"

"Don't play innocent with me, Jacob. What was it you thought I had left behind this morning?"

"Nothing important. By the way, I went to the Pike Place Market today and picked up some nice fresh salmon for dinner. Wait until you see what I can do with a salmon. It's close to miraculous. You're in for a treat tonight."

"Uh-huh. I can't wait." Emily turned in her seat, intent on pinning him down but they reached the garage just then, and Jacob was suddenly very busy using the automatic opener and parking the car.

"By the way," Jacob said casually as he walked her toward the elevators, "the police phoned earlier. They've picked up a couple of suspects who fit my description of the two Morrell sent after me. I'm going to take a look at them tomorrow. Looks like a sure thing, though. Apparently one of them has already started talking. He never met Morrell. Everything was handled over the phone, but the evidence is building."

"I'm so glad they've caught those two!" Emily exclaimed, momentarily sidetracked. She remembered her initial question as they walked into her apartment. "Jacob, I would like to know what you think you were doing following me this morning."

"I'll get the wine," Jacob was saying, going past her into the kitchen. "I've got some chilling in the refrigerator. Oh, I also made the salad. All you'll have to do tonight is sit back and relax."

"Sounds great," Emily said smoothly. But there was a militant gleam in her eyes when she kicked off her shoes and walked barefoot into the living room to put her feet up on a white hassock.

"Here you go. Good Semillon Blanc. You're going to love it." Jacob ambled in from the kitchen with a plate of crackers, a glass of wine and a glass of Scotch carefully balanced. Emily let him sit down before she tried again.

"All right, Jacob. Enough dodging." She leaned back in her chair and glared at him through her glasses. "What were you doing in the garage this morning? I want the truth."

Jacob exhaled heavily. "The truth? I was following you."

Instantly Emily bristled. "I knew it! Of all the nerve. Have you been following me down to the garage every morning?"

Jacob shrugged but didn't say anything.

Emily was not placated. "You have, haven't you? Why, Jacob? What in the world did you think you were doing?"

"Looking after you," he admitted. He smiled with fleeting apology. "I can't help it, Emily. It's a hard habit to break. I never have liked the idea of you coming and going in that damned garage, even before I ran into those two punks down there. Furthermore, I wasn't convinced Morrell had really given up trying to find a way to break RI. I had a hunch he might still try something, even if it was just a shot at hurting you. I figured I'd keep an eye on you until we get out of Seattle."

"So you've been following me? Sneaking around behind me? Checking up on me?" Emily was incensed.

"Now, Emily, there's no need to get dramatic about it. I was just watching out for you."

"You sound as if somebody gave you the job of being my guardian angel. Dammit, Jacob, I won't have it. Do you hear me? For the last time, I can take care of myself."

Jacob gave her an oddly straight look. "Want to know something? Lately I've begun to believe you. Where did you learn that trick you used on Morrell this morning?"

Emily had been about to launch into another tirade, but she paused at the question. Then her sense of humor took over. Her eyes sparkled as she smiled serenely at her husband. "I took a class in self-defense along with the class in assertiveness training."

Jacob groaned. "I should have known. What have I let myself in for by marrying you?"

"I thought you liked the idea of me having turned into a woman with a sense of her own power," Emily remarked dryly.

Jacob grinned. "I may have been a little hasty in congratulating you. Power is a dangerous thing in the hands of a woman. Women are so much more subtle than men. You can usually tell what a man will do with power, but you can't always be so certain about what a woman will do with it."

"It will give you something to think about if you're ever in danger of getting bored with marriage."

"I don't see boredom as a problem in this marriage," Jacob said with great depth of feeling.

"Now, about the way you followed me downstairs this morning," Emily began again, not ready to be sidetracked.

"As long as you're not going to let that subject drop, I'd like to point out a little detail you seem to have overlooked," Jacob said, self-righteousness in his eyes.

"What detail?"

"Emily, I came right down after you in the other elevator. I was only a minute or two behind you."

"So?"

"So I was there right from the beginning when you first encountered Morrell. I overheard you ask him what he was doing there, and I heard the whole conversation between the two of you right up to the point where you threw him."

"It's called eavesdropping, Jacob."

"It's called an incredible display of forbearance and patience on my part. You seem to be missing the main point here, Emily, and that was that I let you deal with Morrell on your own, right up to the moment where things turned violent. Hell, I hesitated so long that you were the one who rescued yourself. Don't I get any credit for that? I'm making progress, honey. Two weeks ago I would have been down on Morrell like a rock slide before you'd had a chance to do anything more than say hello."

Emily stared at him. "You were there behind the wall, listening to everything?"

"And gnawing on my knuckles."

"And you didn't come charging around the corner like a bull moose until after things turned nasty," Emily said thoughtfully, thinking about it.

"A bull moose?" Jacob looked offended.

Emily ignored the hurt protest. Her eyes softened. "You know something, Jacob, there may be hope for you yet. It must have taken considerable willpower for you to hold back when you knew Damon was confronting me on the other side of that wall."

"You'll never know how much willpower," he agreed a little grimly.

Emily broke into a sunny smile. "I hadn't thought about it like that. You're right. You are making progress." Then she remembered something and became thoughtful. "You know, I hadn't realized that fall I gave Damon had shaken him up as much as it did until I saw him getting into the back of the police car. He could hardly walk."

"You're a terror, my love," Jacob said smoothly. He patted his thigh. "Why don't you come over here and tell me just how well I'm doing as a husband who's learning to respect his wife's ability to take care of herself?" Jacob put down his Scotch and reached across the short distance that separated him from Emily. He took the wineglass from her and tugged her down onto his lap.

Emily blinked suspiciously at him and then decided not to ask any more questions about Damon's condition that morning when he had been taken away by the police. Jacob's innocent expression did not deceive her. One couldn't tame a wolf completely. She would just have to be contented with a few behavior modifications.

Emily smiled and went willingly to Jacob, her eyes warm and glowing as she nestled happily into his strength. "I love you, Jacob. Even if you are occasionally overbearing and heavy-handed and even if you do tend to be overprotective."

"And I love you, sweetheart, even if you are occasionally reckless and a little naïve and inclined to drive me crazy." He kissed her forehead.

Emily reached up and framed his hard face between loving hands. She studied the tenderness in his eyes that was such a contrast to the rest of him. "I'm so glad the right time and place finally came for us," she whispered.

"It wasn't exactly a matter of fate," Jacob said with a sexy grin. "We both made it happen. I came back looking for you, and you had the good sense to be waiting."

Emily laughed up at him and pulled his face down so that she could kiss him. "From now on we will take very good care of each other, my love."

CARLA NEGGERS CAPTIVATED YOU ONCE— AND SHE'LL DO IT AGAIN

Trade Secrets, Temptation #162, introduced you to one unique Killibrew sister, Juniper. Juniper's dedication to the family business was hardly rewarded—Cal Gilliam, millionaire rogue, snatched the firm right out from under her and forced her to go nose-to-nose with him in combat. No one, however, *made* her fall head over heels in love with the man.

Now in Temptation #190, *Family Matters*, Juniper's strong-minded sister, Sage Killibrew, encounters yet another rogue. It all begins with an urgent telegram from her long-lost grandfather, which lands Sage in hot water not only with her relative but also with the hero and the hero's father! Sage and *her* rogue, Jackson Kirk, have a few family matters to settle before they can stop the feuding and start the loving....

Look for Temptation #190, *Family Matters*. Destined to captivate you in February!

MAIL-IN-OFFER
OFFER CERTIFICATE ✂

I have enclosed the required number of proofs of purchase from any specially marked ''Gifts From The Heart'' Harlequin romance book, plus cash register receipts and a check or money order payable to Harlequin Gifts From The Heart Offer, to cover postage and handling.

002

CHECK ONE	ITEM	# OF PROOFS OF PURCHASE	POSTAGE & HANDLING FEE
	01 Brass Picture Frame	2	$ 1.00
	02 Heart-Shaped Candle Holders with Candles	3	$ 1.00
	03 Heart-Shaped Keepsake Box	4	$ 1.00
	04 Gold-Plated Heart Pendant	5	$ 1.00
	05 Collectors' Doll Limited quantities available	12	$ 2.75

NAME _____

STREET ADDRESS _____ APT. # _____

CITY _____ STATE _____ ZIP _____

Mail this certificate, designated number of proofs of purchase (inside back page) and check or money order for postage and handling to:

Gifts From The Heart, P.O. Box 4814
Reidsville, N. Carolina 27322-4814

NOTE THIS IMPORTANT OFFER'S TERMS

Requests must be postmarked by May 31, 1988. Only proofs of purchase from specially marked ''Gifts From The Heart'' Harlequin books will be accepted. This certificate plus cash register receipts and a check or money order to cover postage and handling must accompany your request and may not be reproduced in any manner. Offer void where prohibited, taxed or restricted by law. LIMIT ONE REQUEST PER NAME, FAMILY, GROUP, ORGANIZATION OR ADDRESS. Please allow up to 8 weeks after receipt of order for shipment. Offer only good in the U.S.A. Hurry—Limited quantities of collectors' doll available. Collectors' dolls will be mailed to first 15,000 qualifying submitters. All other submitters will receive 12 free previously unpublished Harlequin books and a postage & handling refund.

OFFER-1RR

GIFTS FROM THE HEART

from *Harlequin*

FREE BY MAIL With proofs of purchase
plus postage and handling

A. Hand-polished solid brass picture frame 1-5/8" × 1-3/8" with 2 proofs of purchase.

B. Individually handworked, pair of heart-shaped glass candle holders (2" diameter), 6" candles included, with 3 proofs of purchase.

C. Heart-shaped porcelain keepsake box (1" high) with delicate flower motif with 4 proofs of purchase.

D. Radiant gold-plated heart pendant on 16" chain with complimentary satin pouch with 5 proofs of purchase.

E. Beautiful collectors' doll with genuine porcelain face, hands and feet, and a charming heart appliqué on dress with 12 proofs of purchase. Limited quantities available. See offer terms.

HERE IS HOW TO GET YOUR FREE GIFTS

Send us the required number of proofs of purchase (below) of specially marked ''Gifts From The Heart'' Harlequin books and cash register receipts with the Offer Certificate (available in the back pages) properly completed, plus a check or money order (do not send cash) payable to Harlequin Gifts From The Heart Offer. We'll RUSH you your specified gift. Hurry—Limited quantities of collectors' doll available. See offer terms.

301R

GIFTS FROM THE HEART
ONE PROOF
OF PURCHASE

To collect your free gift by mail you must include the necessary number of proofs of purchase with order certificate.